BRIDE FOR

CW00364034

For the sake of his young son Tim, Iseult had agreed to marry Nicholas Veryan, a man she hardly knew. And it was for the sake of the boy, Nicholas insisted, that the marriage must be a real one. But surely Nicholas couldn't expect that of her, when he was so clearly still involved with Joanna Trethowyn?

Books you will enjoy
by FLORA KIDD

PASSIONATE STRANGER

When Sara accepted an invitation to a concert in California she could not have foreseen that as a result she would be swept back two years—to England, to another life, to the time when she was married to Janos Vaszary. Janos, the man who had taken her heart and broken it in two. Was she ever going to be able to forget him?

PERSONAL AFFAIR

Because she felt sorry for her employer, Greg Lindley, whose marriage had ended so unhappily, Margret was anxious for him to marry Laura Spencer whom he loved and who was so suitable. But it didn't seem likely that Laura would look at Greg as long as his cousin Carl was around. Would it make the situation better or worse if Margret tried to encourage Carl herself?

BEYOND CONTROL

Expediency had been the only reason for Kate marrying Sean Kierly, and immediately after the wedding he had taken himself off and for the next two years she had seen and heard nothing of him. Now, in Ireland, she had met him again—and the natural, sensible thing to do seemed to be to dissolve the marriage. But Kate had fallen in love with Sean at first sight and was still reluctant to divorce him. Yet what was the point of clinging to a man who so obviously didn't love her?

WIFE BY CONTRACT

Her marriage to Damien Nikerios had brought Teri position, as the wife of an immensely rich Greek shipping magnate, money, beautiful homes in Greece—and the humiliation of knowing that Damien had only married her as a cover-up for his affair with his father's wife. Yet for the sake of her family Teri had put up with it. But for how long could she stand it?

BRIDE FOR A CAPTAIN

BY

FLORA KIDD

MILLS & BOON LIMITED
15–16 BROOK'S MEWS
LONDON W1A 1DR

First published 1981
Australian copyright 1981
Philippine copyright 1981
This edition 1981

© Flora Kidd 1981

ISBN 0 263 73674 1

Set in Monophoto Plantin 11 on 12 pt.

Made and printed in Great Britain by
Richard Clay (The Chaucer Press) Ltd,
Bungay, Suffolk

CHAPTER ONE

TOWARDS the middle of the afternoon the drizzle of rain stopped. Slowly the grey clouds which had shrouded everything since early morning began to break up and a pale yellow sun shone through them. Silvery ripples streaked the ultramarine blue of the distant sea. Slits of cobalt blue sky appeared between the clouds and, in the river estuary, the mudbanks gleamed yellow ochre in the sunlight.

It was the moment Iseult Severn had been waiting for; a moment to be seized immediately. Wearing a man's paint-spattered shirt open over a dark blue T-shirt, her long legs clothed in patched much-faded jeans, she moved with lazy grace through the kitchen of the stone cottage and out into the closed-in porch which commanded a good view of the estuary. Through three days of rain she had waited to paint the view, to capture on watercolour paper her impression of the meeting of the sky, sea and land, and all her painting equipment was already assembled on the porch.

Standing over a board on which she had stretched the watercolour paper and which was propped up on an old card table, she picked up an ordinary inch-wide house-painting brush, dipped it into the jar of clear water and let blobs of water drip from the brush on to the upper half of the paper. When she had done that she picked up another smaller brush, dipped the tip of it into some cobalt blue paint, which she had squeezed from a tube on to her palette, and very lightly touched the blue tip of the brush to the blobs of water. Immediately the colour ran into the water.

She was just about to put a wash of ultramarine blue on the paper to define the horizon when the sharp yelp of a dog, the screech of skidding tyres followed by the crunching sound of something moving hitting something hard and immovable startled her and she dropped the brush full of wet paint on to the paper, where it made a splash of colour where she didn't want a splash of colour.

As she jumped to her feet the painting board went flying one way and the water jar and tubes of paint went flying the other when the card table tipped over. Tugging the already open porch door open further, she leapt down the steps and ran along the path beside the house, pushing her way past dripping wet overgrown rhododendrons and azaleas. When she reached the driveway she pulled up short. As she had anticipated, a car had skidded on the wet surface of the road and had collided with one of the huge stone gateposts which stood at the entrance to the driveway. There was no sign of the dog.

Iseult approached the car slowly, afraid of what she might find. Stopping beside the nearest door, which was on the passenger side, she took a deep breath, reached out and turned the handle. The door, being heavy because the car was big and had only two doors one each side, swung open easily and she looked inside, noting that the windscreen had suffered when the car had hit the gatepost and was cracked in several places.

A man was leaning over the steering wheel, clutching his head in his hands so that all she could see of him was shaggy grey hair layered to the nape of his neck. He was swearing softly and fluently. Iseult decided that the swearing was a good sign.

'Are you all right?' she asked.

He lowered his hands and turned his head quickly to look at her, and she felt surprise flicker through her. The lean tanned face beneath the thatch of grey hair was younger than she had expected. He wasn't in his fifties or sixties as she had assumed from the colour of his hair but was about thirty-four or five.

'Bloody dog!' he snarled. 'Brown and white spaniel. Is it yours?'

'No, at least....'

'Whose, then?' He rapped the words out. Anger glittered in his dark eyes and tautened his face.

'I'm not going to tell you,' she retorted, offended by his arrogant manner. 'Not until I'm sure of what you're going to do.'

'Is the dog all right?' asked a childish voice from the back of the car and, glancing over the back of the front passenger seat, Iseult looked right into a pair of round black eyes set in a thin triangular face under a mop of shiny black curls.

'I don't know,' she replied. 'He's run away. I

expect he's frightened. Did you get hurt, too?'

'I banged my nose on the seat in front.' The boy, who was about eight years old, rubbed the end of his nose and showed small white teeth with gaps between them when he smiled at her. 'But I don't mind,' he added. 'I'm glad we missed the dog.'

'The windscreen is cracked, the headlights are probably smashed and I expect the fender is bent. I've bruised a couple of ribs, I'm developing a black eye—and all you can say is you're glad we missed the dog!' said the man with heavy irony.

'You might not have been hurt if you'd had your seat belt fastened, 'Iseult said tartly. There was something about him, an insolence which irritated her. He gave her a dour underbrowed glance.

'I may have to inform the police,' he retorted coldly.

'Oh. Why? Surely you're not thinking of blaming the dog for what's happened?'

'You're damned right, I am blaming the dog,' he said grimly, touching his right cheeckbone with the tips of his fingers. It had been cut and blood was oozing down his cheek in a dark red line.

'But the dog isn't much more than a puppy and he can't help being high-spirited,' she said defensively.

'Do you live in the gatehouse?' he interrupted her roughly, jerking his head towards the cottage.

'At the moment, yes, I do.' She found herself talking to his back because he had turned away from her to open the door beside him. 'I think you're the rudest man I've ever met!' she blurted angrily.

'Then you haven't met many, darlin',' he retorted, looking back at her over his shoulder, a taunting grin flashing across his face and, stepping out on to the road, he slammed the door shut.

'I'm Tim,' said the boy. 'What's your name?'

'Iseult.' She spoke curtly because she was still angry and out of the corners of her eyes she watched the man go round to the front of the car, which was wedged up against the gatepost, and bend down to look at the damage.

'Is ... Is ... I can't say it,' said Tim flatly.

'You can call me Isa,' she replied, smiling down at him. He was really very appealing in a foreign way with his dark slanting eyes and curly black hair. 'Most people do. Iseult is an old Cornish name. Hasn't anyone ever told you the story of Tristram and Iseult?'

'No. Is it funny? Would it make me laugh?'

'Not really. It's about King Mark of Cornwall, his wife Iseult and her ...' Iseult realised she was getting into deep water and added lamely, 'her friend Tristram.'

'We're in Cornwall now,' said the boy. 'The school I used to go to is in Devon.'

'Don't you go to it any more?'

'Not since yesterday. He,' pointed in the direction of the windscreen, presumably referring to the man, 'he came and took me away.'

'But surely the summer holidays haven't started

yet. It's only the end of May.' She was suddenly
worried. 'Are you sure he had the right to take
you away? I mean, he hasn't kidnapped you or
anything, has he?' she whispered, stories she had
read in the newspapers about the kidnapping of
children by their own estranged parents flashing
through her mind.

'Oh, no.' The boy's grin bore a resemblance to
the man's. 'You are funny,' he added with a
chuckle of infectious laughter. 'He's my father,
and he was angry because they ... the people at
the school ... were nasty to me. So he took me
away. And now we're going to our house.'

'Where is that?'

'At the end of the driveway. We were just
coming round the bend in the road and the flicker
was on to show we were going to turn left when
your dog ran out in front of us. Dad wasn't going
to stop, but I shouted, "Mind the dog!" and he
braked and we skidded and *bump*, we hit the gatepost.'

'You live at the Captain's House?' Iseult
exlaimed, and when he looked puzzled she explained quickly, 'I know Linyan is the real name
of the house, but everyone around here and in
Polruth has always called it the Captain's House
because Veryans—that's the family who always
owned the house—went to sea and were captains
of ships.'

'He owns the house now Grandfather is dead
and he goes to sea and is now a captain on a ship
... a big tanker.'

'I see,' said Iseult slowly. She was beginning to realise why the man seemed familiar to her. 'Look, Tim, would you like to come into the cottage with me and have some biscuits and milk? I have to tell my mother about the accident.'

'Will I see the dog?' he asked.

'You might if he comes back soon.'

'All right, I'll come.'

He pushed forward the back of the front passenger's seat and scrambled out of the car on to the road. He was a sturdy boy with broad shoulders and long legs and he was wearing grey flannel shorts, a grey shirt and a navy blue v-necked pullover, which Iseult supposed was his school uniform.

They went round to the other side of the car where the man was standing scowling down at the broken headlight, bent fender and dented bonnet of the car. The man looked up his dark eyes narrowing as their glance flicked over Iseult assessingly, making her feel very much aware of the untidiness of her appearance, her old painting clothes, her blonde hair, roughly cut by herself, falling forward in her eyes and swinging past her cheeks. She probably had smudges of paint on her face too. Whereas he looked neat and elegant in well-cut dark grey pants and a v-necked cream-coloured cable-patterned sweater which he wore without a shirt.

'Your'e Iseult Severn,' he said abruptly.

'That's right.' Her chin lifted and her eyelids dropped over her amber-coloured eyes as she took offence at his cool, insolent manner.

'It's been a long time since I last saw you.
There've been some changes.' Again his dark
roving glance made free of her appearance and
she felt her blood boil.

'I don't think we've ever met,' she retorted.

'We've never met face to face like this, and we
were never formally introduced,' he replied. 'But
I used to see you often enough, about ten years
ago when I was home on leave one summer.'

Ten years ago she had been thirteen, a long-
legged teenager without a care in the world, and
he had been about twenty-four, tall, broad-shouldered and slimmer than he was now, with a lot of
silvery blond hair going dark at the roots, giving
an attractive piebald effect. The only son of
Matthew Veryan, one-time master mariner in the
Merchant Navy, he had driven a battered sports
car too fast about the twisting country roads that
summer and had played the devil with the local
girls. He had behaved as the Veryans had always
behaved, according to the stories which had been
told over the years about his ancestors, like a lord
of all he had surveyed; like a bold buccaneer
taking whatever he had fancied even if it had
belonged to someone else. That summer he had
taken her brother Tristram's girl-friend Joanna,
and Tristram had been very hurt for a while.

'I didn't recognise you at first,' she said coolly.
'You've changed too, Nicholas Veryan.' Her
glance went deliberately to the prematurely grey
hair. She supposed the blond hair, instead of

changing completely to darker brown, had lost the little colour it possessed and had become grey. But far from ageing him the colour made him even more attractive, contrasting with the deeply tanned skin, black eyebrows and dark eyes. 'That cut on your cheek is bleeding quite a lot,' she added. 'You'd better come into the house and bathe it.'

She didn't wait to see if he would follow her and Tim. With the boy she pushed her way past the wet bushes to the back of the house. Up the steps to the porch she went, Tim close behind her. She stepped over the fallen card table and so did Tim. At the back door of the house, which was slightly open, she stopped and looked round to see if Nicholas Veryan had come. He entered the porch, surveyed the mess and bent immediately to pick up the card table.

'Please leave it,' said Iseult. 'I'll put everything straight later. I knocked it over when I heard the dog yelp.' She stared at him accusingly. 'You know, the car must have hit Merlin for him to yelp like that.'

'The car hit the gatepost, not the dog,' he retorted dryly. 'And now I know who owns the dog. Only Win Severn would give a dog the name of the magician in the legend of King Arthur in the same way she named her two children after two characters in a Cornish myth.' Again the dark eyes raked her from head to foot. 'Last time I was home and talked to Win she said you were studying art in France and she was expecting you to marry one of your art teachers. Is that why you're here? Have you come home to be married in Polruth Parish church?'

'No. I'm not getting married here . . . or anywhere else,' she retorted stiffly. She knew she had gone white and she had difficulty in forcing the words out, her throat was so dry.

He made no comment, but after giving her another calculating glance which seemed to strip her of everything he bent and picked up her drawing board. Holding it before him, he studied the smudged and ruined watercolour, the taunting curve of his mouth becoming more pronounced.

'Are you trying to follow in your father's footsteps?'

'I paint sometimes, but not like my father,' she replied tautly.

'I agree with you,' he murmured, still looking at the painting. 'He's good,' he added aggravatingly, and put the board on the table.

'Oh!' she gasped, and turning quickly pushed her way into the kitchen. Adrenalin was pumping through her veins, causing her heart to beat faster, tautening her muscles and making her ears sing. With anger expressed in every abrupt and noisy movement she made, she took out the biscuit tin, poured milk into a mug for Tim and told him to sit at the table.

'Do you have something I can clean this cut with?' asked Nicholas, and turning to look at him she found him peering in the small mirror which hung above the sink. The blood was dripping from his face now and the right eye was half closed by the swelling around it.

'If you'd like to sit down I'll clean it for you,' she offered, knowing she sounded reluctant and ungracious but unable to speak to him differently.

To her surprise he did what she had suggested, pulled out a chair from the table and sat down. Iseult found the first aid box, filled a bowl with warm water and taking a pad of cotton wool dipped it in the water and bent towards him. Obligingly he tipped the right side of his face up towards her.

His eyes were indigo blue, she realised, so dark they were almost black, yet under the tan caused by exposure to wind and sun his skin was that of a fair-haired person. He was the mixture often found in that part of the country where the darkness of the original inhabitants had been overlaid by the blondness of later invaders and immigrants. There was something Middle Eastern about his profile. His forehead was broad and sloping, his nose took a bold downward curve and his lips had a sensual curve to them, like the lips of the statue of a Greek god she had once seen.

She hadn't been so close to a man since Pierre had held her in his arms and had made love to her. Her hand shook suddenly and uncontrollably and she jabbed the corner of the cotton wool pad into the corner of Nicholas's eye.

'Hell!' He flinched back from her, his hand going up to cover his eye.

'I'm sorry.'

'What's the matter with you? Why are you so nervous and uptight?' His uncovered eye glared at her angrily. 'You're not going to tell me you've never been this close to a man before?'

'There's nothing the matter with me,' she lied. 'If you'll take your hand away I'll put ointment on the cut and cover it with a plaster.'

When she had pressed the plaster firmly against his tanned cheek she stepped back from him with relief, inwardly amazed at her own awareness of his physical appearance. He meant nothing to her. In fact she didn't like him and had never liked what she had known about him, and she had a sensation of having collided with him in much the same way as his car had collided with the gatepost; a head-on collision which had not only made her angry but had aroused her senses to an unusual awareness.

'Would you like a cup of tea?' she asked, closing the first aid box with a snap. After all, he might be suffering a little from shock.

'No, thanks. But I would like to see Win, since she owns the dog. Is she at home?'

'She's in the studio. I'll go and get her,' she said, glad of an excuse to get away from him. She was part way along the passage which led to the studio when she realised Tim was with her.

'Do you think the dog will come back soon?' he asked.

'He might be back already and be in here,' she said, pushing open the door of the studio.

It was a high, wide room, and had been specially designed by Mark and Win Severn. All one wall was made up of windows through which it was possible to see the curve of the green lands sloping down to the river. In one corner was the printing press where Mark produced the etchings for which he was deservedly well known. In another corner was the pottery wheel where Winifred Severn was sitting forming a bowl from wet clay. Shelves on the other three walls were stacked with artist's materials, canvas, papers, paint, books, pottery bowls and vases waiting to be decorated and fired. A plain wooden stairway led up to a gallery which was cluttered with easels, mores canvases and more paint.

'What's up?' Winifred asked when she saw Iseult and Tim. A fairly tall woman, with greying fair hair cut very short, she had finely chiselled features and clear grey eyes. Like Iseult she was wearing jeans over which hung a brightly patterned smock.

'Merlin got out and ran into the road,' Iseult replied.

'And?'

'Nicholas Veryan swerved to miss the dog, but his car hit the gatepost.'

'Oh, God!' Winifred sighed exasperatedly, and switched off the wheel and began to wipe her clay-covered hands with a cloth. 'Is he hurt?'

'Who? Merlin or Nicholas Veryan?'

'Both, I suppose.'

'The dog ran away,' said Tim, and Win's eyes

widened when she looked at him.

'How like Rosita he is,' she murmured. 'But I suppose that could only be expected.'

'Who's Rosita?' asked Iseult.

'His mother,' said Win vaguely. 'What damage was done to Nick?'

'He has a cut on his cheek, a black eye and says his ribs feel bruised. Mother, he's threatening to tell the police it was Merlin's fault.'

'How did the dog get out?'

'I must have left the back door open when I rushed out on to the porch to paint. The rain had stopped and the clouds were just lifting and I had to try and catch the moment. The porch door was also slightly open.' Iseult smiled ruefully. 'I'm sorry, Mum, I forgot about Merlin.'

'Will the dog come back soon?' Tim asked. 'I want to see him.'

'I think he's back now. Listen,' said Win. From the outer door of the studio came a sniffling, whining sound.

'Can I let him in?' whispered Tim, his eyes shining.

'Of course you can.'

As soon as the door was open the dog bounded in, tail wagging, claws scrabbling on the floor as it wriggled its hindquarters in pleasure to be home. Its usually creamy white and brown hair was plastered with mud.

'You've been in the river again, I see,' said Win. 'Here, Merlin, come here and let me look at you.' Under her firm but gentle hands the dog lay quietly on the floor while she felt its limbs and body. 'There doesn't seem to be anything broken. You've had a narrow escape, Merlin. I hope you realise it and behave in future. Nick Veryan doesn't usually stop for anyone and it doesn't do to get in his way.'

'Your opinion of me is interesting, Win,' said a quietly ironic voice from the house end of the studio, and they all turned their attention from Merlin to Nicholas, who was standing in the other doorway. As he came into the room the dog scampered over to him, tail wagging ecstatically.

'You stupid hound!' Nicholas snarled softly as the dog licked his hand. 'Don't you recognise me as the heartless driver to whom your owner has just referred? You should growl and snap at me.' He gave Win a level critical glance. 'You haven't trained him very well,' he rebuked her. 'He has no road sense yet. Why don't you keep him tied up when he's out of doors and unattended?'

'Because I couldn't do that to a dog,' replied Win coolly.

'It was my fault he got out,' said Iseult. 'I didn't close the back door properly and I didn't see him go. If I had I'd have gone after him and called him back.'

'I guessed you might be at fault,' he remarked dryly, and her breath hissed as she drew it in sharply. She had a great urge to slap his lean cheek.

'You were driving too fast,' she accused. 'And

if you had any road sense yourself you'd have slowed down sooner for the bend in the road. Then you wouldn't have had to swerve to avoid Merlin and you wouldn't have skidded on the wet road and hit the gatepost. You're more to blame for the accident than the dog is. And if you report the dog to the police I'm going to report you for lack of due care when driving with a child in your car!'

'So there,' he mocked, his grin taunting her.

'I told you you were going too fast, Dad,' said Tim with a deep sigh as he sat down on the floor beside Merlin.

'Ha, ha!' Win's chuckle of laughter was delighted. 'You're condemned, Nick—out of the mouth of your own babe. And you have to admit you haven't got a very good record with the police of this county when it comes to speeding. Another offence and they might take your licence away.'

'All right, you win. I'll let your dog off this time,' said Nicholas, giving his son a murderous glance before raising his eyes to stare narrowly at Iseult again. 'But if he dashes in front of my wheels again you can be sure I won't swerve to avoid him.' He paused and turned to Win, and his grin lashed out. 'And then you'll be able to pride yourself on having assessed my character correctly,' he added.

'Are you home for long?' she asked, smiling back at him, obviously liking him.

'For as long as it takes me to find someone to look after Tim,' he replied, frowning. 'I had to leave the ship and fly back when I received a message from the headmaster of the preparatory school that he was having problems. I'm not due for leave yet, was hoping to take it in July and August when my present commission ends so I could be with Tim in the summer holidays.' He paused, then asked, 'You wouldn't know of anyone who could look after him for a few weeks, I suppose, a good housekeeper-nanny type?'

'No, I don't. Have you advertised?'

'Several times before this. No one wants to live at Linyan. They all say it's too remote. Yet I feel he'd be happier living there and going to the school in Polruth.' His mouth quirked in self-mockery. 'We Veryans don't take kindly to being institutionalised.'

'I agree, he would be happier here,' said Win.' 'And if I do hear of anyone who would be suitable I'll let you know.'

'Thanks. How's Mark?'

'Fine. He's away in London at present, putting up an exhibition of some of his prints.'

'And your business here? Is it going all right?' Nicholas glanced at the rows of hand-thrown pottery bowls and jars.

'We're looking forward to a good summer season and have many commissions for pottery. Iseult is going to help me while she's here. Do you think your car will go? Has any damage been done to the steering or the engine?'

'I'll soon find out if there has,' replied Nicholas. 'Come on, Tim, let's get going.' He moved towards the door of the studio.

'I want to stay with the dog,' said Tim.

'You'll come with me,' said Nicholas, his voice silky with menace. 'Look sharp now. On your feet!'

'Oh, all right.' Tim drew a sigh again as he stood up and went over to the door. 'Can I have a dog of my own now I'm going to live at Linyan?'

'We'll see.' From the open doorway Nicholas looked back at Iseult. 'Thanks for being an angel of mercy,' he said, his eyes glinting with mockery as he touched the plaster on his cheek. 'I realise you were reluctant.'

'Tell Tim he can come any time to see Merlin,' Win said.

'I will,' he said, and closed the door.

Iseult let out a long hissing breath.

'He's ... he's an....' She bit back the words with which she was going to describe Nicholas in deference to her mother. 'He's insufferable,' she added lamely.

'Who is? Nick? Or the boy?'

'Nicholas.'

'Well, he's certainly stirred you up,' remarked Win. 'For the better too. You look less of a ghost of your former self, and it makes a nice change to see some colour in your cheeks and to know you can still get angry. Nick always makes me think of a slap of cold salt water, he stings but he refreshes too, makes me perk up as he's made you perk up. What do you find insufferable about him?'

'Everything.' Iseult paced up and down the room, hands in the front pockets of her jeans. 'Mostly the way he speaks to Tim.'

'Seems to me he handled the boy pretty well, considering he's never seen much of him. At least Tim will know where he stands with Nick. It takes a Veryan to control a Veryan and always did.'

'But Tim is like his mother, you said so yourself.'

'In looks. She was a Brazilian, had that lovely golden skin and Indian-dark hair and eyes. But I could see by the way Tim was looking around here that there's plenty of the Veryan devil in the boy, and I wouldn't be at all surprised if Nick was asked to take him away from the school because he was in trouble.'

'What happened to Tim's mother?' asked Iseult.

'She was drowned, near here.'

'In the sea?' Iseult exclaimed, her eyes wide.

'So it was decided at the inquest when her body was washed ashore. She'd been missing for a while. Everyone thought she'd left Nick and had gone off with another man. Nick didn't bring her to live at Linyan until about five years ago when Tim was three. Until then she'd lived in Rio, where Nick met her. She was a strange person, didn't fit in too well with the way of life here.'

'Who looked after Tim after she'd gone away?'

'Matthew, Nick's father, and his housekeeper. that arrangement came to an end when Matthew died last year and Miss Tremayne, his housekeeper, decided to retire. That's why Nick sent Tim to a private preparatory school where he could live in. I believe Mary, Nick's elder sister, keeps an eye on him while Nick is away, and has him for holidays.'

Win rose to her feet and stretched her arms above her head.

'I think I've done enough work for today,' she said. 'Let's go and make a meal. I'm starving!'

CHAPTER TWO

TEMPERAMENTAL as always the Cornish weather changed again in the night. The wind backed to the south-west, the sky became overcast with clouds again and even as Iseult looked out of her bedroom window while she rubbed the sleep from her eyes the first rain came softly—nothing much, she thought, a fine drizzle which might clear later as it had the day before. But by lunchtime she had to admit that her prediction had been wrong. Gradually the rain had increased to a slanting steady fall that meant another day indoors, helping Win to paint designs on the pottery bowls and vases.

About three o'clock Tim arrived. Wearing a yellow raincoat, a sou'wester on his head and wellington boots on his feet, he grinned up at her

when she answered his knock on the studio's outside door. He'd come, he said, to take Merlin for
a walk and hoped she would come too. Iseult
looked at the rain, looked back at the black eyes
gazing up at her so appealingly and gave in, and
for half an hour, with Merlin on the end of a long
thin rope, they shuffled together through the
shrouded gloom of the Linyan woods.

Every afternoon for the next four days, which
were all wet and windy, Tim came in the afternoon to walk with Isa and the dog and to return
with her to the gatehouse for milk and biscuits
before going back to Linyan House, where, he had
told her, his father was busy decorating the hallway and the dining room.

'I try to help him,' he confided with a sigh to
Iseult. 'But I don't like the smell of paint. It makes
me sneeze all the time.'

'I thought you were going to go to school in
Polruth,' Iseult commented.

'That's next week, I start on Monday. But I'll
still be able to see you and Merlin. I can call in
after school. The bus stops just by the gatehouse.'

At last, on Saturday morning, the weather
changed for the better. The day dawned in a sun-
shimmered haze and Iseult knew it was going to
be one of those days of delight which she had
known as a teenager when she had first come to
live in Cornwall. The sun would shine and it
would be a good time for her to go to Polruth to
sketch the harbour. Perhaps later she would ride

round the head of the harbour to the other side
and walk along the cliffs beyond Potter's Pyll and
watch the sea surging among the rocks.

She made some sandwiches and a flask of coffee
and packed them with her sketchbook and camera
into a canvas bag which she could sling satchel-
wise over her shoulder, then, after telling her
mother she would be gone for the day, she set off
on her old bicycle pedalling slowly up the hills
and free-wheeling down the other sides of them,
feeling her spirits soar in a way they hadn't soared
since she had left Paris. Perhaps the time spent
here in the country living with her placid indus-
trious mother was having a beneficial effect at
last and she was beginning to recover from the
shock inflicted on her tender sensibilities by
Pierre Boudreau, one of the artists with whom she
had been studying and whom she had hoped one
day to marry.

Yet would she ever forget the cold horror and
shame she had experienced that afternoon when
arriving unexpectedly at Pierre's studio she had
found him making love to another woman, to
Marie St Aubin, an artist's model who had often
posed in the nude for the life-drawing classes
offered by the Académie de St Lazaire. Even now
as she cycled up the last hill between her and
Polruth she could feel that awful sickness clawing
at her stomach which she had felt when she had
seen Pierre's hands caressing Marie's bare olive-
tinted skin.

She had rushed from the studio without a word

and for the next few hours had wandered about the streets of the Left Bank, blind and deaf to all that had been going on about her. If she had been a different person, if she had been cool and hard like her room-mate Alex Johnson, a truly liberated woman who was able to treat sex like a man, as something she had to have and without becoming emotionally involved, she would not have been so shocked. But she had not been like that, nor would she ever be like that. Sex for her was a part of love, and she had loved Pierre and had believed he loved her, so that seeing him with Marie had shocked her almost out of her mind.

Somehow she had eventually found her way back to the apartment she had shared with Alex, had packed her cases and had left a note for Alex saying that she had decided she had studied for long enough in Paris and was returning home. She made no attempt to see Pierre because she hadn't wanted to hear him lie to her in defence of his actions. Thoroughly disillusioned, she had realised that for him she was not the woman he loved most in all the world, as he had often told her, but was just another female whom he could manipulate to satisfy his desires and that his suggestion that she should marry him one day had been a trick, his way of persuading the shy and innocent person she was to capitulate to his experienced lovemaking.

Her parents had accepted her return from the Paris academy of art where she had been studying for almost two years without comment and to her great relief had never questioned her about the breaking up of her relationship with Pierre. Her father had suggested that she stay with them for a while to help Win in the studio, decorating the pottery, polishing stones to be set in the Celtic type jewellery Win made, and helping him to make prints of local scenes which were all sold in the small gallery that they owned in Polruth, during the summer season.

But it hadn't been easy to recover. Many a night had been sleepless as she had wondered whether she had overreacted when she had run away from Paris and as she suffered from withdrawal symptoms from the idea of being married to Pierre. She had wanted to be married, had longed to have that intense yet loving relationship which her mother had with her father. Now it seemed she would never have it, because after seeing Pierre with Marie she felt she would never trust another man sufficiently to agree to marry him.

She reached the top of the hill and paused to get her breath, looking down at Polruth, a small port which had once exported china clay and had been renowned for its fishing fleet. Both industries had declined and although there was still some fishing done Polruth had joined many other Cornish towns and had become a tourist attraction and a centre for artists. Shark hunting, waterskiing and underwater fishing were all offered, as well as a few charter sailing boats.

Built on the slopes of the Linyan peninsula, its old stone houses seemed to slide down the narrow

streets to the pool-like harbour. Iseult rode out to
the wharf where a few small fishing boats were
tied up, propped her bike against the wall, found
a pile of fish boxes on which to sit and was soon
busy sketching.

She sketched quickly everything she could see;
the boats moored in the middle of the harbour;
the seagulls circling and screeching about the
fishing boats where someone was gutting fish and
throwing the entrails into the water; a group of
fishermen standing talking; lobster-pots, nets,
coloured buoys. At the end of an hour she had
several sketches from which she could make
paintings and she decided to take some photographs to go with them.

'Isa, Isa, what are you doing?' She recognised
Tim's voice at once, and after taking a final snap
of the harbour she turned to see him coming towards her along the wharf. He was dressed in
denim dungarees and a checked shirt over which
he wore a zipped windbreaker.

'I'm taking photographs. What are you doing
here?' she asked.

'We've come to go sailing in one of those boats.'
He pointed to the sturdy old-fashioned wooden
day boats which could be rented for a few hours.
'Dad says he'll show me how to sail and we'll
have a picnic over there.' He waved a hand in the
direction of the opposite shore which glimmered
green and yellow through the bluish morning
haze. 'Come with us, Isa.'

'I'd like to come, but I think it would be best if

I waited for your father to invite me. He might
not want me to go with you,' she replied, looking
beyond him at the blue car parked at the other
end of the wharf. Nicholas was taking something
out of the boot. It was a sailbag. He put it on the
ground beside him, looked round and shouted,

'Tim, come here. You can carry the picnic
basket.'

'I'll ask him if you can come,' said Tim, backing
away from Iseult in the direction of the car.

'No, Tim, please don't,' she said hastily, but he
ignored her plea and dashed back to the car.

Iseult turned away and raised her camera to her
eye to take another photograph of the fishing
boats, not because she needed one but to cover
her embarrassment at the thought of Tim asking
Nicholas if she could go with them, wishing she
could vanish into thin air somehow. She would
have liked to have gone sailing, but she didn't
want Nicholas thinking she had suggested to Tim
that they take her with them. She supposed she
could walk back to her bike and ride away, but to
do that she would come face to face with Nicholas
as he came along the wharf on his way to the
rowing dinghies which were clustered together at
the bottom of the stone steps leading down to the
water from the top of the wharf, and she didn't
want to do that. Oh, what was the matter with
her? Why couldn't she treat Nicholas Veryan as
he treated her—coolly, as if he didn't matter to
her, because he didn't?

She lowered the camera and looked across the

harbour. The haze was clearing as a breeze ruffled the water and the sands and cliffs beckoned invitingly. It would be much more pleasant to sail there than to cycle round by the road; to skim over the sparkling water, to feel the breeze in her hair and the sting of salt water on her skin.

'Isa, Dad says you can come if you want.' Tim was at her side again. He was carrying a wicker picnic basket and was slightly out of breath.

She looked round. Nicholas had walked past her and was going down the steps to the dinghies, the sailbag slung over one shoulder. He hadn't stopped to ask her if she would like to go with them but had issued a careless indifferent invitation through Tim, giving the impression that he didn't care one way or the other if she did go with them.

'Please come with us, Isa. I'd like you to come. It'll be more fun if you do.'

Tim was looking appealing again. He was much more charming and persuasive than his father was, and yet there had been a time when Nick Veryan would have turned on the charm too. Iseult had seen him do it ten years ago, with Joanna, persuading her to go with him instead of going with her brother.

'All right, I'll come since you ask me,' she said. 'I'll just go and lock up my bike.'

Nicholas was squatting on the bottom step holding the edge of one of the small dinghies and Tim was sitting in the bow, nursing the picnic basket when she joined them.

'Tim has invited me to go with you,' she began to explain, talking down to the top of Nicholas's navy blue yachting cap.

'Do you know anything about sailing?' he interrupted her curtly, glancing up at her. The plaster had gone from his cheek and there was only a thin red mark there. The swelling had gone down about his eye although the skin was still bruised and greenish looking.

'Yes, I know something about sailing,' she replied stiffly. 'But I'm not coming. . . .'

'Oh, Isa, you said you'd come,' complained Tim, moving forward from the bow of the dinghy so that the little boat rocked precariously.

'I told you to sit still!' Nicholas barked at him, and glanced up at Iseult again. With his black eyebrows slanting in a frown he looked extremely bad-tempered. 'Get in, and sit in the stern,' he ordered.

'It's obvious that you don't want me to come,' she began again, her pride up, tilting her chin, causing her eyes to sparkle. She pushed her thick, straight blonde hair back from her face. 'And I don't go where I'm not wanted.'

'What I want is immaterial,' he replied dryly. 'Tim would like you to come and you told him you would, so get in and sit down.'

She was tempted to turn and walk back up the steps, to show him he couldn't order her about as if she were one of the seamen on a ship, but a glance in Tim's direction made her hesitate. The boy was tightening his lips as if to prevent them from trembling and she noticed the sudden sheen of tears in his eyes. She could hardly disappoint him now, so putting a hand on Nicholas's shoulder to steady herself, she stepped into the dinghy and sat on the stern thwart. Immediately Nicholas followed her, sat on the centre thwart and soon he was rowing the boat away from the wharf.

Over the shining water the dinghy slid, oars dipping and rising rhythmically, towards the nearest of the day boats. When they were on board the bigger boat Nicholas told Tim to stow the picnic hamper under the cuddy or shelter in the middle of the boat while he hoisted the mainsail, which was already tied on the boom. Then he showed Tim how to clip the foresail, which he had brought with him in the sailbag, to the forestay. When both sails were flapping idly he took hold of the tiller and asked Isa to go forward and cast off the mooring buoy. The sheets were pulled in. The sails filled with wind, the little boat heeled and moved forward through the water.

The sun was warm, the water glittered and the only sound was the slap of waves against the bow as the boat floated across the harbour, tacking back and forth against the light wind until it was over the bar. Then Nicholas ordered the sheets to be freed and the boat surged forward in the direction of glinting granite cliffs topped with grass and stunted trees which had been blown backwards by the persistent south-westerly gales so that they looked like so many umbrellas blown inside out.

'We'll go to Potter's Pyll,' said Nicholas. He lounged at his ease on the cockpit seat with the tiller under his arm, his eyes lifted to the luff of the sail. A navy blue crew-necked fisherman's jersey drew attention to the powerful column of his sun-tanned neck and the wide bulk of his shoulders while his faded blue sailcloth trousers were shaped by his sinewy thighs and legs. Aware that she was staring at him too long and becoming too interested again in his physical appearance, Iseult looked away over the lee rail of the boat where the water foamed and chuckled.

'I used to go there with my brother Tristram and his friends,' she replied coolly.

'How is Tris? I haven't seen him for years.'

'Very well. You know, I suppose, that he emigrated to Canada?'

'Win told me. Which part is he working in?'

'He's working for an oil company, surveying in the Arctic looking for more oil,' she said, raising her hands to hold her hair on either side of her head. Thick and straight, it resembled a mop and had a way of blowing forward to cover her face whenever she was out in the wind.

'In the Beaufort Sea?' Nicholas's manner changed from one of casual indifference to interest.

'I think that's the name of the place,' she said.

'I was in the Arctic last August,' he said. 'At Melville Island. The Canadian tanker I was on was the first to make a commercial trip through the north-west passage from east to west. We delivered jet fuel to an exploration base on the island.'

'Were you the captain of the ship?' she asked.

'No. Second mate. But after that trip I was able to get a captain's berth with another shipping company and I've been going back and forth to the Persian Gulf for the past few months. And I hope to continue as a captain now I've had the experience and if I can find someone to look after Tim.'

Iseult was about to ask him why he didn't ask his sister to take care of Tim while he was away at sea, then changed her mind. It was his problem and nothing to do with her, so she stayed silent and looked away at the sea, which was now a hazy aquamarine flecked with golden light stretching away to a smudged violet horizon like a Turner painting. Turning to look over the other side of the boat, she saw water surging in sparkling foam against dark jagged rocks.

It was past one o'clock when they reached the almost landlocked haven of Potter's Pyll or Pool and ran in behind the reef of rocks which sheltered it from the swell of the sea. Nicholas rounded the boat up in the small shallow pool until the sails flapped. After asking Iseult to hold the tiller and keep the boat head to wind he ran forward and dropped the anchor, coming back to lower the mainsail.

All was quiet save for the cry of birds on the shore. Looking over the side of the boat into the few feet of water, Iseult drew Tim's attention to some regular flat stones, dark and grey under the water. They were the remains of the old jetty which had once jutted out from the shore.

In the tiny dinghy which had been towed behind the day boat Nicholas rowed Tim and Iseult ashore. They beached the little boat on the firm wet sand of the shore and tied its painter round a convenient rock. Oyster-catchers, disturbed by the invasion of humans, took off, flashes of black and white, swooping to a more remote shore, with strange flute-like cries. Smaller redshanks and sanderlings scurried away to probe scattered slaty rocks. The faint breeze whispered a last song in the sea-rushes, planted long ago to hold the sand together, then died away completely and all was quiet again.

After eating the sandwiches they had brought and drinking the tea and milk, they all walked up the shore to follow the path which led to the end of the rocky headland. Keen to sketch, Iseult found a place to sit. Nicholas and Tim disappeared over the edge of the cliffs, presumably to look at the next bay, a rocky indentation on the coastline known as Marriott's Cove.

'I like the way you draw, Isa,' said Tim.

Finishing her third sketch, she looked round to find him at her shoulder looking at the sketch pad. There was no sign of Nicholas.

'Where's your father?' she asked.

'He's gone down the cliffs and he's walking along the beach on the next bay. It's very rocky and I couldn't keep up with him. Anyway, I'd rather be with you.' He smiled at her seraphically. 'Will you draw me?' he asked.

'If you can sit still.'

'Where shall I sit? Is this all right?' He sat down cross-legged on the grass a few feet away from her.

'That's fine.' She began to sketch the shape of his head with quick strokes of charcoal.

In looks he was like his mother, Win had said. Had Rosita had a softly rounded face, and silky black curls? What had she really been like, Nicholas's wife? And why had she left Linyan? Because she couldn't live with Nicholas any more? Because they had been incompatible? Strangely, as she sketched Rosita's son, Iseult felt very close to the woman. It was as if Rosita was there, somewhere, beyond the edge of the cliffs. Iseult shook her head sharply, to shake the feeling off. She wasn't normally given to believing in ghosts or the supernatural, although living in Cornwall with its strange, wild history it was easy to become fascinated by the haunting past.

'Are you looking forward to going to school on Monday?' she asked. Talking to Tim, who was very real, would keep her mind off Rosita.

'Yes. It'll be much nicer than going to the other school 'cos' I'll be able to go home every day instead of staying in a stuffy dormitory with the other boys. At home I have my own room with my own things in it,' he replied, then sighed. 'But I wish Dad didn't go to sea. I wish he'd live at Linyan all the time so I can always go to school at Polruth.'

'Maybe he'll find someone to live at Linyan and look after you,' she murmured comfortingly.

'Did you know, Isa, that some of the Veryans were pirates long ago?' he said, changing the subject completely. 'Dad says there are cellars under the house where some of them who were smugglers used to hide the smuggled goods. I wanted him to take me down into the cellar, but he won't. One day I'm going to find the door to the stairs and explore the cellars myself.'

'Perhaps he won't take you down there because it isn't safe to go,' said Iseult. 'I've heard a story about a maid who once worked at Linyan and she went down into the cellar and couldn't get back into the house because the door had locked itself. So she tried to find her way out by the tunnel which led from the cellar to the shore, but the tide came in and she was drowned. So it isn't a good idea for you to go down there by yourself. You might not be able to get back into the house.'

'I wish you lived at Linyan with us,' was Tim's next surprising remark, and she gave him a quick wary glance. He returned her look with an angelic smile. 'Wouldn't you like to live there, Isa?' he persisted. 'If you could look after me I wouldn't mind about Dad going to sea. He could marry you and you could be my stepmother. It would be better than having a housekeeper-nanny person.'

Iseult stared at him incredulously.

'But I'm not old enough to be your stepmother,'

she argued weakly.

'What's age got to do with it?' he retorted. 'It's liking that counts,' he added with a wisdom which seemed far beyond his years. Forgetting he was posing for her, he rolled over on to his stomach, cupped his chin in his hand and kicked his legs in the air. 'It's hard being an unwanted child,' he said with another sigh, giving her a bright shrewd glance from under his lashes.

'I'm sure it isn't true, that you're unwanted,' she said quickly.

'Yes, I am. No one wants to look after me. I used to go and stay with Aunt Mary and Uncle Peter in the holidays from the other school, but they've gone to Australia and I can't go all the way there. And Dad says he can't give up going to sea to stay and live with me all the time because it's in his blood or something and he likes going. And my mother didn't want me or she would have taken me with her when she went away.'

'Oh.' Iseult felt a little shock of surprise because he didn't seem to know that his mother was dead. 'Do you remember her?'

'Sometimes I think I do. She looked a little like me and she had a lot of black hair and big black eyes. She used to hug me. She used to cry a lot, too.'

'If she hugged you she must have wanted you and loved you,' Iseult suggested gently.

'If she'd wanted me she would have taken me with her when she left Linyan,' he argued stubbornly, scowling at her.

Iseult didn't disagree with him this time. She looked up at the sky. The sun had moved round to the west and the shadows of the trees and the rocks were lengthening already. She glanced at her watch and wasn't surprised to see that it was almost half past four. Closing her sketchbook, she pushed it into her canvas bag.

'The tide must have turned by now and it's time we started to sail back to Polruth,' she said. 'I wonder where your father is?'

They wandered over to the other side of the headland and looked down to the rocky beach of Marriott's Cove which curved round to another steep-sided promontory pitted with the dark opening of caves. There was no sign of Nicholas on the beach and Iseult felt suddenly anxious about him. Marriott's Cove was not one of her favourite places. With its dark granite ledges slanting down to the sea and its echoing caves, it possessed a brooding atmosphere, and she knew from reading local history that in the past ships had been wrecked there and many people had been drowned.

'Where do you think he is?' asked Tim.

'I don't know.'

'I hope he hasn't fallen on the rocks and hurt himself,' he said, sliding a hand into hers for comfort.

'Let's shout his name and see if he appears,' suggested Iseult.

They both cupped their hands about their mouths and shouted as loudly as they could.

Blackheaded gulls nesting among the cliffs soared up screeching noisily in reaction, but as far as Iseult could see Nicholas did not appear on the beach.

'I'll go down to the beach and walk along it and shout to him,' she said.

'But you might fall and hurt yourself,' Tim said anxiously.

'No, I won't. I'll be very careful. You stay here and look after my bag. You can watch me all the time. I'll keep looking back at you and I'll wave to you and then you'll know I'm all right. I'll walk as far as those caves. Your father might be exploring in them.'

She went down the winding path which twisted down the cliffside between clumps of furze bushes. Once she was on the beach she cupped her hands around her mouth and shouted again. Behind her the cliffs sent back her voice in echo, 'Nicholas, Nicholas!' No one answered her, but the gulls soared up again in noisy protest and circled above her.

Turning, she set off in the direction of the caves, stepping from rocky ledge to rocky ledge carefully, pausing sometimes to look curiously into the sea-water pools caught among the rocks, slipping occasionally on the seaweed which festooned the ledges. Several times she stopped and shouted, then turned to wave to Tim as she had promised, waiting for him to wave back before she went on.

She had almost reached the first cave and had

turned to wave to Tim when she heard rocks scrabbling against each other as if someone walked over them, and looking round she saw, with a sensation of relief, Nicholas walking towards her.

'Looking for me?' he asked coolly as he came up to her. He had rolled up his pants to calf level and his sailing shoes, which he wore on bare feet, were soaking wet. In his dark fisherman's jersey with the yachting cap rakishly aslant on his head he resembled one of the pirates or smugglers Tim had been talking about.

'Yes, I am,' she retorted, irritated by his coolness. 'Where have you been?'

'Examining the caves. Looking for evidence,' he replied shortly, glancing past her to the solitary figure of Tim standing on the headland.

'What sort of evidence? Evidence of smugglers?' she asked.

'No.' He paused, his lips twisting into a bitter line. 'Evidence of death,' he added sombrely, and she felt her flesh creep.

'Whose death?' she whispered.

'Rosita's,' he replied with a heavy sigh, then added by way of explanation, assuming that she didn't know whom he was talking about, 'My wife was called Rosita. She disappeared from Linyan four years ago. A few months later her body was found washed up on this beach.'

'I see. I'm sorry,' she muttered, remembering with a tingle of apprehension the strong feeling she had experienced when sketching Tim that Rosita had been near at hand, just over the edge of the cliff. She looked round searching for something to talk about, to change the subject, and her eye was caught by the glint of granite walls through the foliage of the usual masses of wild rhododendrons on the land which sloped up from the beach. 'Does anyone live in that house?' she asked.

'Not all the time. It's a cottage belonging to distant relatives of mine. You might know their son, Charles Marriott. He used to go about with your brother when he was down here on holiday.'

'I didn't know the Marriotts were related to you.'

'Charles is a cousin several times removed,' he remarked dryly.

'I think we'd better get back to the boat,' she said. 'It's after four-thirty and the tide has turned.'

'So I'd noticed. I had to wade back from the farthest cave.' He slanted her a sardonic glance from under the peak of his cap. 'Were you worried? Is that why you came looking for me?'

'Tim was worried. Didn't you wonder why he wasn't with you?'

'I knew he'd gone back to you. He told me he was going back.' His dark glance lifted to the wind-blown mop of her bright yellow hair and his mouth curled mockingly at one corner. 'He seems to have formed quite an attachment to you over the last few days. At first I thought it was the dog which attracted him to the gatehouse, but now I realise it's you.'

'Well, don't let that give *you* any ideas,' she retorted, remembering uneasily Tim's suggestion that she should marry his father and become his stepmother, and, turning away from Nicholas, she began to walk back over the rocks towards the path which led up the cliffs.

CHAPTER THREE

'IDEAS about what?' asked Nicholas, catching up with her and walking along beside her, his wet shoes squelching as he stepped from rock to rock in lithe easy strides.

'About asking me to look after him so you can go back to sea,' she replied lightly.

'How did you know I was thinking of asking you,' he asked. 'Did Tim say something about it?'

About to leap from the rock she was on to another, Iseult changed her mind and turned to look at him. He stood before her, hands rested easily on his hips, and once again she experienced the feeling of having collided with him, his physical appearance had such an impact on her.

'You're not taking him seriously, I hope,' she said. 'I mean ... boys, all children take sudden likings to people they've never met before and don't know very well,' she muttered.

'I am taking him seriously,' he interrupted. 'And I've been thinking it over most of the afternoon, wondering what would be the best way to approach you. By bringing the matter up yourself you've precipitated it somewhat. I was going to wait a few days, until you and I had got to know each other a little better. On the other hand, you've saved me some trouble, and the important point is not whether you and I like each other, but that Tim likes you and you seem to like him.'

'I suppose you think I've nothing better to do than to be a housekeeper-nanny to an eight-year-old boy,' she challenged.

'I don't think that way at all,' he retorted. 'Nor does Tim. But I've come round to agreeing with him that the only way to solve the problem is for me to marry again and provide him with a stepmother.'

'Oh no,' she said flatly. 'Marriage is out of the question. I can't marry you.'

'Why not? You're not still engaged to the artist in Paris.'

'I wasn't engaged to him,' she said through stiff lips.

'But you're not going to marry him.'

'No, I'm not.'

'Then you can marry me.'

'No, I can't,' she cried rather wildly. 'I don't want to marry you. I'm not in love with you and....'

'Were you in love with him?'

'Yes,' she whispered the word.

'Then why didn't you stay with him and marry him?' he challenged her.

'I don't want to talk about it,' she evaded, and would have leapt down to the next ledge of granite, but he caught hold of her arm. 'Let go of me!' she said angrily, pulling her arm free of his grasp. 'Don't touch me!'

Nicholas's eyes narrowed speculatively and he folded his arms across his chest.

'It would be better for you if you did talk about it,' he suggested curtly. 'You've been hurt, and a hidden wound often festers and causes trouble later.'

'Well, I'm not going to talk to you about it,' she retorted.

'Okay, you don't have to.' He shrugged. 'But you can listen to the rest of what I have to say. I wasn't thinking of a love-match. Marriage for so-called romantic love ... whatever that may be ... doesn't necessarily work out.' His mouth twisted cynically. 'I'm approaching it as a business arrangement. I know you're out of work. . . .'

'I'm not. I'm working for my parents.'

'And they aren't really in a position to employ you to play at painting pretty pictures,' he jeered.

'I do not play at painting pictures. I paint quite well and I'm very good at making prints and decorating pottery.'

'But you're not good enough yet to sell anything you make and support yourself financially,' he replied. 'You still have to work for someone else.'

'It takes years to become established as an

artist, that's why.'

'Just as it's taken years for Mark and Win to become established in their own fields of art, yet still they're not making much money. Still they're poor and in debt.'

'In debt to whom?' she demanded in surprise.

'To me, for one. They're way behind in their mortgage payments on the gatehouse.'

'But I thought they owned the place now. I thought they finished paying the mortgage some years ago,' she exclaimed.

'They took out a second mortgage three or four years ago, to finance your art training in France.'

'I won a scholarship to the Académie de St Lazaire,' she retorted.

'Granted, but I suspect that only paid your tuition fees,' he pointed out. 'You still needed money for food and lodgings and for travel, didn't you? And who provided that? Mark and Win, of course, and the only way they could raise the money was to mortgage the gatehouse, and since no building society would let them have a loan on the house, because it's so old, my father lent them the money. They're still paying the interest on it.' His hard glance raked her. 'And now you've come back to sponge on them,' he added nastily.

'I'm not sponging on them. I'd get a job if I could, but you must know how hard it is to get any sort of decent employment just now.'

'And that's why I'm offering you a job now, as stepmother to Tim,' he countered determinedly. 'All you would have to do is live at Linyan House, look after him, see that he goes to school every day, be there when he comes home in the evening, attend to his clothes, give him some of the attention you've been giving him the past few days, and in return you would have a roof over your head, financial security and the freedom to paint your pictures, make your prints and decorate the pottery. You won't get a better offer anywhere, and it's worth thinking about.'

'But I'm not going to think about it,' she replied spiritedly. 'Because I don't like you, and I don't like your cold-blooded arrogant approach to marriage.'

'Would you prefer it if I made up to you, pretended to be in love with you, kissed you and fondled you as I guess the Frenchman did?' he remarked unpleasantly, and she gave in at last to the urge to slap him, raising her hand and swinging it wildly at his face. He moved quickly, his hand flicking out to catch her wrist, his fingers curling about it tightly.

'Not in front of Tim,' he said softly. 'I don't want him to be upset by any violent behaviour on your part.'

Slowly, his glance holding hers, he let go of her wrist, his fingers sliding from it almost caressingly, their tips lingering lightly on the thin delicate skin over the pulse so that she felt a delicious tingle shoot along her nerves.

'Dad, Isa—come on!' Tim's voice rang out clearly from the top of the cliffs. 'I want to go sailing again.'

'You'll have to find someone else,' Iseult whispered, still staring at Nicholas, trying to pretend his touch on her wrist had not affected her. 'Or give up going to sea and stay at home to look after him yourself.'

'I can't afford to give up going to sea,' he replied. 'A captain's pay is good and it enables me to keep Linyan House. If I didn't go to sea I'd have to sell the house and move to a city, to find some sort of job, and since I'm not trained to do anything but navigate ships it wouldn't be much of a job. As for finding someone else, why should I? You're here, on the spot. You like living here and would like to stay. You've no money, and what's most important, I know your background. I know you're made of sound, wholesome stuff, even if you are an artist.' He smiled suddenly, right into her eyes, and she caught her breath at the glimpse of a different Nicholas, the charming if rather wild young man who had conquered Joanna Trethowyn. 'You'll think about it,' he added softly, 'because you're already tempted to accept my proposal. You won't be able to stop yourself thinking about it.' And turning on his heel he strode away over the rocks towards the cliffs.

By the time they all reached the beach at Potter's Pyll the water was creeping up the shore and around the dinghy. There wasn't much wind and the sails flapped uselessly on the day boat, but, caught on the flooding tide, the boat drifted towards the entrance of Polruth harbour.

Since they were moving slowly Nicholas threw mackerel lines astern, tying them to cleats on the boat, and told Tim to watch them. Determined to ignore both of them, Iseult stared towards the Linyan peninsula which jutted out into the sea to form one side of the harbour. Covered in newly-sprouting grass and unfurling bracken, dotted with furze bushes, it glowed green-gold in the rays of the westering sun and as it came closer she could see, peeping above the ridge, two square chimneys and the slanting slate roof of Linyan House.

For a long time the boat sat on the flooding tide at the entrance to the harbour, and only by patient and skilful handling of sails and tiller could Nicholas manage to coax it over the bar and in the direction of its mooring. Tim wound in the lines. On one of them hung a limp dead fish. Polruth's many windows brimmed suddenly with golden light, then went dim suddenly as the sun slid behind a wooded hill on the western shore. The water shimmered silver. The boat slid sideways to its mooring. Nicholas handed her the tiller and went forward to lift the buoy on deck.

It was a moment of satisfaction and tranquillity, this return to harbour, thought Iseult as she sat leaning on the tiller while Nicholas and Tim stowed the sails. Although they had been away only seven hours and had sailed only about ten miles she felt she had been on a long voyage and was now enjoying the repose of journey's end. Or it would have been repose if she had not been so disturbed by Nicholas's suggestion that she should marry him.

'What's the matter, Isa?' Tim demanded as they went ashore in the dinghy. 'Didn't you like going sailing with us?'

'Yes, I liked it,' she replied coolly.

'Then why are you so quiet?'

'Because I've nothing to say,' she said with a little laugh.

'Will you come with us again to-morrow?'

'You might not be going again to-morrow,' she replied. 'It might rain again.'

'Dad, did you ask her?' Tim leaned forward urgently to whisper loudly in his father's ear.

'Sit still,' ordered Nicholas curtly. 'Never move your weight about violently in a small boat like this. You upset the trim of it when you do and could swamp it.'

'But did you ask her?' persisted Tim as he sat back in the bow.'

'Yes, I did. And she's going to think about it.' Even in the twilight Iseult could see mockery dancing in his dark eyes as he looked at her. 'Aren't you, my darlin'?' he added tauntingly, and she knew he used the endearment in the West Country way, casually, not meaning anything, and all she could do was to lift her chin and turn her head to stare at the jumbled cottages and twisted streets of the town where lights were already twinkling, like yellow stars.

They wouldn't let her ride home on the bike because the light was going and the bike had no lamp, no rear light and no reflectors. Somehow Nicholas managed to tie it on to the back of the car and she sat in the front passenger seat next to him. When they arrived at the gatehouse he untied the bike and lifted it down for her. She said goodbye to Tim and as the car drove away up the driveway and wheeled the bike round to the back of the gatehouse and put it in the gardening shed.

There was a small Volkswagen parked at the back of the house and she knew her father was home. She found him and her mother in the comfortable untidy living room sitting on the chintz-covered sofa holding hands as they talked. It was a sight which had welcomed her home often.

'I was just thinking of sending out a search party for you,' Win joked as, after kissing her father, Iseult sank down in her favourite chair on the opposite side of the old Cornish hearth which took up most of one wall of the room.

'I met Tim and Nicholas in the village and they took me sailing with them. We went to Potter's Pyll. There wasn't much wind and it took us hours to get back. How are you, Dad? How was the exhibition? Did you sell any pictures?'

'Three, and received enquiries about some others. Jack Holmes and Anna Wells who were also exhibiting did quite well, too.' As always Mark was diffident about any success he might have achieved. 'So you've been hobnobbing with the Veryans today, have you? I thought the boy was at a private boarding school.'

'Nick had to come home because the boy was in some trouble at school. The other boys were tormenting him, apparently, because he's a little bit different,' explained Win. 'Tim has become an admirer of Merlin and of Isa and he comes here every day.'

'I made some sketches and took lots of photographs,' said Iseult quickly, determined to direct the conversation away from the Veryans. She got to her feet and went over to the canvas bag which she had dropped by the door, picked it up and took it back to her chair. From it she took her sketchbook and handed it over to her father. 'I thought I might be able to do some small paintings. Local landscapes often sell in the summertime.'

Her diversion worked. For the rest of the evening they talked about art and the Veryans were forgotten, but as soon as Iseult was in bed both of them stepped right into her mind again. *She's going to think about it, aren't you, my darlin'?* Nicholas's words returned to mock her. Here she was thinking about his suggestion, weighing the pros against the cons. Mostly there were pros, she discovered. Marriage to him would be advantageous to her. She would be able to stay in this area; she wouldn't lack for anything; she would have time to paint and help her parents in their art business. It would be advantageous to Tim too. A business arrangement—how cold it sounded, how unromantic. And yet ... she fell asleep suddenly, contentedly weary after her day in the fresh air.

During the next few days she saw nothing of Nicholas, but she thought much about his proposal of marriage, especially after Tim had called in to see Merlin on his way home from school in the afternoon. Every day the boy asked her if she had been to see Nicholas and was always disappointed when she said no, she had been too busy helping her mother or painting pictures to go visiting.

'He says I'll have to go to another boarding school if he can't find anyone to look after me soon,' said Tim in a shaky voice as they returned from their usual walk through the woods with Merlin. 'I wish you'd say yes, Isa. Why won't you say yes? Don't you like me?'

'Yes, I like you . . . but . . . oh, it's hard for me to explain to you. Your father asked me to marry him and I . . . I'm not sure whether I can.'

'Don't you like him?' persisted Tim.

'I. . . .' She broke off to look down at him. The big black eyes held a stricken expression and she squatted suddenly to put her arms about him. 'Oh, Tim, don't look like that! It'll be all right, I promise you it will. You won't have to go to boarding school again. We'll work something out, I'm sure.'

'You'll go and see Dad tomorrow, then?' he whispered. 'He says if he hasn't found an answer by Saturday he's going to take me to see the headmaster of another school he's heard about farther away from here, in Dorset. And I don't want to go away from here. I like being here and taking Merlin for walks and seeing you ... and Win and Mark. I like the school here and Miss Leigh, my teacher. Isa, promise you'll go and see Dad tomorrow?'

'I promise,' she said.

All evening she thought about the matter, so absorbed in her thoughts that although she knew her father was talking to her at one point she didn't hear a word he was saying.

'Isa.' His usually quiet voice was suddenly sharp. 'What's the matter with you? You aren't listening.'

'I'm sorry. I was thinking.'

'Obviously.' His voice was dry.

'Something worrying you, Isa?' Win's voice was more gentle.

'Tim is,' she said briefly. 'He told me today that his father hasn't found anyone to look after him and so he's going to send him to another boarding school. He's very unhappy about it.' She paused, then said quickly before she could change her mind, 'Nicholas has asked me to marry him.'

There was a short silence while they both stared at her. Mark's eyes, heavy-lidded and golden-brown like her own, held a thoughtful expression while he puffed at his pipe. Win's expression was one of frank amazement for a moment and then changed to one of twinkling amusement when she laughed.

'My God, I always knew Nick Veryan was a fast worker—but not that fast! He's been here barely two weeks and in that time as far as I know you've seen him twice,' she remarked. 'Unless you and he have been meeting in secret?' she added.

'No. I haven't seen him since last Saturday when he made the suggestion. He said it would be a business arrangement. Tim would like me to look after him and it would be easier for me to do that if I were his stepmother.'

'So now we know why you've been absent-minded recently,' murmured Mark. 'You're tempted to accept his proposal, aren't you?'

'Yes, I am.'

'On the rebound?' asked Win shrewdly.

'What do you mean? Rebound from what?' Iseult exclaimed.

'From your affair with Pierre. When you were home at Christmas you were all excited because you were going to marry him. Four months later you return home, down in the mouth about something, with not a word about getting married to Pierre, and now you're thinking of marrying a man you don't know very well. Sounds like a case of rebound to me.'

'Well, it isn't. If I marry Nicholas it won't be for love. It will be for Tim's sake,' retorted Iseult sharply. 'And there's a lot to be discussed before I come to a decision.' She paused, looking from Win to Mark and back to Win again, seeing for the first time the lines on their faces which anxiety had etched there. 'Did you really borrow money from Matthew Veryan to finance my going to Paris?' she asked.

'Did Nick tell you about that?' said Mark.

'Yes.'

'We did borrow from Matthew,' said Win. 'But why should Nick tell you about that? He isn't using the fact that we still owe the Veryan estate money to pressure you into marrying him, is he?'

'No. At least not in the way you're thinking. He isn't going to foreclose on the mortgage if I don't marry him,' replied Iseult. 'He was just pointing out that you two have supported me long enough. And he was right—you have. It's time I was supporting myself financially. Only it's so hard these days to find a decent job, even when you've been well educated and have specialised.'

'Nick may have been right,' said Win angrily, 'but he shouldn't have said that to you. You're our daughter and what we do for you is our concern.' She paused and stared at Iseult, comprehension dawning in her eyes. 'Good God,' she whispered, 'you wouldn't marry him just to gain financial security, would you, Isa?'

'I might,' replied Iseult lightly. 'and it wouldn't be the first time a woman had done that, would it?'

But discussing the matter with her parents had churned up her mind and she had little rest that night as she tussled with her conscience and her principles. Next morning was fine, with sunshine filtering through the mist, and after giving Win some help Iseult decided to take her watercolours and her sketch pad and walk through the woods to the shore below Linyan House.

The view was one which she had always liked.

Rock-scattered sands curved round to a well-known headland on which a lighthouse flashed its warning and, since the day was still misty, sounded its foghorn at regular intervals. She found a convenient place to sit on the small canvas stool she had brought and was soon putting washes of colour on her pad. As always when painting she became oblivious to everything except the shimmer of sunlight through the mist and the sparkle of the waves as they tumbled on the sands.

'Do you know you're trespassing?' Nicholas spoke behind unexpectedly. She jumped and her brush fell from her hand and rolled across the pad of paper, leaving splodges of bright Cadmium yellow paint wherever it touched.

'Oh, you've ruined another painting!' she exclaimed, swinging round to face him.

'I have?' His glance went to the wet paper. 'Perhaps it's just as well I did speak to you,' he added mockingly. 'It was a mess before you dropped your brush.' Glinting with derision, his dark eyes lifted to her face. 'You're easy to surprise.'

'Well, wouldn't you jump if someone crept up behind you and spoke suddenly?' she retorted.

'You've got paint on your nose,' he murmured irrelevantly, sitting down on the grass beside her.

'And you've got it in your hair,' she countered, looking down on the thick thatch of grey strands so close to her elbow.

'That's not surprising really,' he replied. 'I've

been painting the ceiling of the entrance hall of the house. Would you like to come and see what I've been doing? You can compare my painting with yours, then.'

'Yes, I would,' she said without hesitation, acknowledging to herself that her reason for coming this way was to see him. She had hoped he would see her from the house and would approach her, because it was time she gave him an answer to his proposal.

Down the slope they walked to a stream which wound between stunted willows towards the sea. Across the clear tumbling water they went by way of stepping stones and up the other side through a meadow starred with daisies and buttercups to a gate set in a dry stone wall behind which rhododendrons crowded, their thick leaves dark green and spiky spreading out under huge purple pink blooms.

The front of the house was long, facing a lawn edged with flower beds crammed with perennials. The walls were granite and sparkled in the sunlight. It was a very plain house, built in simple early Georgian style with five sash windows in the upper storey and four on the ground floor, two on either side of the front door. Virginia creeper, its new leaves fresh and green, fluttered against part of the front wall.

The door was open and they stepped into the square hallway, which had a staircase with a carved wooden banister. Part of the hallway was panelled in dark oak which had been intricately

carved with garlands of roses. Between each
wooden panel the plastered wall had recently been
stripped of paper and now gleamed with ivory-
coloured paint. The ceiling had also been painted
ivory.

'There was wallpaper on the plaster panels,'
Nicholas explained. 'Stripping it off was like
stripping off cardboard, there was so many layers.
Underneath the walls were pretty smooth, so I
decided to paint. Makes the place much lighter,
don't you think?'

He showed her the other rooms on the ground
floor, the sitting room, wide and long, which had
an elegant Adam fireplace, and the dining room
furnished with a long refectory table and carved
chairs. In the study they lingered while Nicholas
showed her the models of sailing ships which his
father had made and which were all in glass cases.

'These are all ships which the Veryans either
owned or sailed on in the past,' he said. 'He made
this room a sort of memorial to the family.' His
mouth quirked with sardonic humour. 'My
mother used to hate this house. She said it was
too full of the ghosts of bygone Veryans for her to
live here comfortably. That was why she left.'

'Where does she live now?'

'In Switzerland. As far away from the sea as
possible,' he replied dryly. 'Rosita didn't like
being here, either,' he added.

Iseult glanced at him quickly, sensing he had
been hurt because his wife hadn't liked his home.
Eyebrows slanting in a frown, he seemed to be

looking into the past.

'I didn't know your parents were separated,' she said.

'They were divorced, eventually,' he said abruptly. 'Mother married again. I can't really blame her for leaving him when she did. He was a very difficult man to live with and was almost twenty years older than she was. She didn't leave until Mary and I were grown up and could fend for ourselves, so there was no squabbling over the custody of children. Nor could either of us accuse her of abandoning us. Let me show you the kitchen.'

At some time quite recently the big kitchen had been modernised and it was equipped with a big electric cooking range, stainless steel sinks, a washing machine and a dryer.

'All this electrical equipment is all right as long as there isn't a south-westerly gale and the electric power isn't cut off,' said Nicholas. 'Then we have to go back to the old days and light oil lamps and candles and cook on the Cornish hearth there.' He pointed to the old structure built into the thickness of the wall of the house, the oven being at the back of the fireplace and covered by an oval door.

'It's very like the one at the gatehouse,' remarked Iseult.

'And is all that's left of the original house built on this site. I suppose you know that the first Linyan House was destroyed by a rather disreputable ancestor of mine, John Veryan, when he was entertaining some of his more piratical friends to an orgy one winter's night.'

'I had heard that story. Wasn't he the man who murdered his brother's son after his brother had been presumed lost at sea so he could inherit the house instead of the boy? But his brother came back and found out about the murder.'

'That's right. So John got drunk, and set fire to the house. The elder brother, the one who came back, Ralph Veryan, built this house for his second wife.' Nicholas's mouth twisted cynically. 'He was also a smuggler, but a respectable one, if that's possible, and it was he who had the tunnel made from the seashore to the cellar and had the secret door to the cellar stairs designed.'

'How does the door open?' she asked.

'There's a spring lock. You have to know which panel and then which rose on that panel contains the spring lock.' He leaned against the kitchen table and folding his arms across his chest, looked across at her challengingly. 'Well, now you've seen most of the house, do you think you could live in it?'

Iseult looked around the kitchen. All she had seen of the house she liked. It had an elegant simplicity that appealed to her.

'I could live in it,' she replied.

'And not be afraid of its ghosts?'

'I don't believe in ghosts,' she replied lightly. 'Couldn't your mother look after Tim for you?' she asked.

'I wouldn't ask her. I want him to grow up in

this country, preferably here at Linyan where I grew up.'

'But Tim says you're going to send him to another boarding school.'

'That will only happen if you refuse to be his stepmother,' he replied coolly. 'I'm hoping you're going to give me an answer this weekend. If you say no, I'll have to send him to another boarding school, because I have to rejoin my ship in two weeks' time. The compassionate leave I was granted to come home and deal with him will be up then.'

'He's very upset at the thought of going away to school again.'

'I know he is, but there's nothing I can do about it, and he won't have to go away if you'll agree to marry me before I go back to sea.'

'But there isn't time for us to marry before you go. It takes three weeks.'

'I could get a special licence, I'm sure, considering the circumstances, and we could be married in Polruth Parish Church,' he replied calmly.

From under her lashes Iseult studied his face. There was no softness in it. He was a determined, ruthless man and she found herself wondering how Rosita had dealt with his ruthlessness. But then perhaps Rosita hadn't come up against it. Perhaps he had behaved differently to her, had made love to her and persuaded her to do what he wanted with kisses and caresses. *Would you prefer it if I pretended I was in love with you, if I kissed you and fondled you as I guess the Frenchman did?*

His mocking remark echoed through her mind, startling her. Was that what she wanted? Would she have preferred that approach to this cold no-nonsense slightly cynical approach? Oh, no, surely not, after her experience with Pierre.

'You're Tim's choice, Iseult.'

Nicholas had come across to her, was standing very close. With her head bowed all she could see of him was the taut stretch of the material of his paint-spattered shirt across his broad chest and the dark hairs showing where the shirt was unbuttoned. He smelt of sweat and turpentine, hardly a romantic combination of smells, but they were going to her head, making her senses reel and tingle with awareness of his powerful masculinity.

'And I really believe he would have more sense of security if he lived with someone he likes and who he knew was legally related to him,' he went on reasonably. 'What's the problem? What's making it difficult for you to decide?' he added.

You are. The words screeched through her mind, but she did not say them aloud.

'I have to know what else you would require of me before I decided,' she said quickly, looking up at him. 'As a ... as a wife, I mean,' she added as he frowned in puzzlement.

His frown faded and his dark eyes glinted mockingly.

'I wondered when we'd get round to that,' he murmured. 'I shall require all the usual services, of course,' he went on. 'It won't be one of those paper marriages.' He drew in his breath impatiently, the frown returning. 'But I'm tired of this haggling. You know the situation. I spelled it out pretty clearly to you at Marriott's Cove last week. I'll give you until six o'clock Saturday evening to make up your mind, one way or the other. If you haven't accepted my proposal by then I'll go ahead and make arrangements on Sunday for Tim to go to another boarding school when I go back to sea about two weeks from now.'

'Oh, he'll be so mixed up with all this changing of schools,' she protested. 'And I think you're very selfish putting your career before him.'

'Frankly I don't give a damn what you think of me,' he retorted coldly. 'And both he and I would starve if I didn't put my job first. But if you're really concerned about what happens to him you'll take my offer and marry me to provide him with a stepmother he'll like. You'll take it as it stands or you'll leave it. And if you haven't turned up here by six tomorrow evening I'll know you've decided to leave it.'

'If I feel the way I do now I'll probably leave it,' she flung at him, and whirling round, she made for the back door, tugged it open, stepped outside and slammed it shut.

She marched quickly down the winding driveway past the high bank of rhododendrons. All desire to paint had gone, and once again she felt as if she had been in collision with a rugged

immovable object. She felt bruised mentally.
Nicholas Veryan was an arrogant, self-centred
male chauvinist who didn't care if he hurt other
people as long as he got his own way, and she
couldn't possibly marry someone like that.

But what would happen to Tim if she didn't?
The question bothered her all afternoon as she
helped Win to wrap up pottery bowls and vases
and place them in boxes in readiness for their
conveyance to St Ives the next day.

'Angela would like to have them when she
opens her arts and crafts shop for the summer
season on Monday,' Win explained. 'I'm driving
over there tomorrow morning. Would you like to
come with me? You could take a couple of those
watercolours you've done. She might be interested in them and sell them for you.'

'Oh. Do you think so?' said Iseult, diverted at
last from the problem of Tim. 'Then I'll certainly
come with you.'

CHAPTER FOUR

THE white mist which had shrouded the coast
thinned and dissolved to reveal the woods and
fields of the river valley as Win and Iseult drove
towards St Austell next day. When they reached
the town Win chose to take a secondary road that

lifted over the long backbone of Cornwall, crossing a high plateau of land encompassing White Moor and Hensbarrow Downs; the china clay country.

It was a fantastic, alien world, very different from anywhere else in the Duchy. High greyish-white pyramids formed from the waste matter left over from the quarrying of the clay gleamed against the pale blue sky. At the bases of some of them unused pits had filled with water which glinted ice green in the sunshine. It was a beautiful world where man had dug for a living from the granite for generations, leaving nature to decorate the waste he had made in her own way. Wild flowers straggled across the waste, adding delicate touches of colour, and wandering birds from the moorland skimmed over the pools.

Dipping down from the plateau, the narrow road joined the main road which links the rest of England to Land's End and turning left, Win drove south-west towards Truro and Redruth.

'Something on your mind?' she asked. Iseult had sat so far in silence, looking out at the scenery.

'How did you guess?' she replied lightly.

'You keep sighing. And normally you aren't so quiet.'

'I'm worried about Tim.'

'Why?'

'Yesterday Nicholas issued an ultimatum. He said that if I haven't agreed to marry him by six o'clock this evening he's going to send Tim to another boarding school.'

'Mmm. He's certainly applying pressure, isn't he?'

'And I hate him for it,' muttered Iseult vehemently, and felt rather than saw Win's quick glance in her direction. 'And how can I marry someone I hate?' she added.

'Hate is a strong word, and I wouldn't have thought you were capable of hating anyone.'

'Well, he rouses strong feelings in me. He's ... so hard and arrogant. If he'd approached me differently I might have agreed to marry him before now.'

'If he'd wooed you, you mean?' queried Win. 'I doubt it. I can imagine you would have repulsed him and hated him even more. Since breaking with Pierre you've been very much on the defensive.' She paused, then added thoughtfully, 'And there is another way of looking at it. Supposing Nick had taken a different approach and had soft-soaped you into marrying him and later you'd discovered he hadn't meant a word he had said, you would have even more cause to hate him and would perhaps walk out on him, something he doesn't want to risk happening because of Tim. You ought to be glad he's been honest with you and hasn't made any pretence of being in love with you.'

'You're always on his side,' Iseult grumbled.

'No, not always. Nick and I have had our disagreements, but I think I understand him better than you do.' Win paid attention to her driving for a few minutes, then continued, 'He took a beating, emotionally speaking, when he found out that Rosita had apparently left him before she was found drowned. He changed a lot, grew a protective shell and became very wary of emotional involvement with women. I suspect he's found it difficult to come out of that shell, lower his pride and admit he needs to marry again for Tim's sake, and that's why he's been cool with you.'

'But I've always disliked him, ever since he stole Joanna away from Tris,' Iseult complained. They were approaching the town of Hayle with its old iron foundries, at the head of the estuary of the Hayle river. Once the river had been broad and deep, a natural entrance for the ships that had come trading not only from Ireland but also from the Mediterranean. Now it was silted up and sand dunes crowded about the narrow channel marked with poles to warn any seamen of the ever-encroaching sandbanks.

'Joanna Trethowyn, you mean?' asked Win as she turned the car off the road to Land's End and drove along another which curved beside a wide bay. 'Tris went about with her years ago.'

'Ten years ago, to be exact. And he was very fond of her.'

'But he was never serious about her. They were both only about nineteen and he was still a student at Southampton University.'

'Tris was serious enough,' retorted Iseult. 'And then Nicholas came home on leave and took over. I saw it happen one evening when we were all at

Polruth summer fair. Honestly, Mother, he turned on the charm and within seconds she was walking away from Tris with him. She never bothered with Tris after that, and he was very hurt.'

'But not for long. And she was no loss,' said Win dryly.

'Oh, why do you say that? She was very pretty and lively,' protested Iseult.

'And had an eye for the boys, or rather the men. Joanna was promiscuous and her grandmother had a terribly worrying time with her, never knowing where she was on those short summer nights or who she was with. She was probably quite happy to go off with Nick that night, to make love somewhere. He'd be much more attractive to her than Tris was at that time. Nick was older, more mature, more experienced, and he had money in his pocket. Later she went to London, you know, to be a fashion model there, and found herself a wealthy protector whom she married eventually.'

'Does she ever come back to Polruth?' asked Iseult.

'She was here a few years ago when her grandmother died. She owns The Gables, the house in the High Street where her grandmother used to live. It's divided up into flats, you know.' Win changed gear to take a steep incline in the road. 'But you should forget about Joanna, and you shouldn't dislike Nick for taking her away from Tris.' She glanced sideways at Iseult. 'I think you're just using that as an excuse. It's really Nick's indifference to you that you dislike. You know very well he would never have considered asking you to marry him if it wasn't for Tim, so your pride and vanity are stung.'

'That isn't true,' said Iseult spiritedly, but for the rest of the drive she was quiet, wondering secretly if her mother was right.

Soon they were in St Ives and driving down one of the precipitous streets to the waterfront where Angela Winter, a long-time friend of Win's from art college days, had her arts and crafts boutique, overlooking the famous horseshoe-shaped harbour which in the past had dominated the fishing industry of the north coast of Cornwall.

Angela, small, plump and vivacious with sparkling black eyes and greying black hair, was in the little shop waiting for them and they were soon busy carrying in the boxes of pottery, un-wrapping the contents and setting the bowls and vases on the shelves in the storage room at the back of the shop. After that was done Iseult brought in the two watercolours she had painted and which Mark had framed for her the previous night. Angela studied them critically.

'They're not quite in the same style as Mark's, are they?' she commented eventually. 'But that's to be expected, since you're a different person and see everything differently,' she added quickly, smiling encouragingly at Iseult. 'I like them,' she went on firmly. 'They're fresh and youthful and represent scenes which anyone could recognise. They're the sort of thing a tourist will often buy to take home as a memento of a visit to Cornwall. I'd like to buy these two and see how they sell. If they sell quickly I'll be back to you for more.' She smiled again. 'How much?' she asked in her crisp businesslike way.

When the sale was completed and Iseult had Angela's cheque in her handbag, making her feel on top of the world because for the first time she had sold something she had created, they all went in the Volkswagen up one of the steep streets and along a road which curved westward along the cliffs to the cottage where Angela lived with her elderly mother, and two Siamese cats and where they sat down to a long, very filling lunch.

Since Angela and Win seemed disposed to talk for the rest of the afternoon Iseult went out for a walk, climbing a path through the furze and bracken to the top of the cliffs from which she had a magnificent view of the bay and the jumble of roofs, chimneys and church towers of St Ives.

It would have been in such a place that the *huer* or lookout had stood to watch for the shoals of pilchard fish, years ago, she thought. He would have been armed with a furze bush and, as soon as he had seen the dark cloud of fish rippling the smooth water of the bay, he would have waved his bush either to the right or to the left, indicating the progress of the shoal to the fishermen on the shore waiting by their boats. And he would have shouted '*hevva, hevva!*' the word meaning shoal of fish from which the word *huer* had been derived. The boats would have been launched immediately and thousands of the shimmering, leaping fish, slightly smaller than herrings but bigger than sardines, would have been trapped in the nets.

But for some reason the pilchards had stopped swarming into the bay and for years now St Ives had been known principally as a centre for artists and, instead of fish, tourists swarmed through it in the summer months, crowding its narrow streets, filling the fishing boats to go sport fishing for sharks or just for trips around the beautiful bay.

Iseult took several photographs of all she could see and made a few sketches and then walked back to Angela's house. Win and Angela were still chatting in the sitting room while old Mrs Winter nodded sleepily in her chair by the window.

'It's five o'clock, Mother,' Iseult announced pointedly. 'Don't you think we should be going home?'

'Oh, not yet,' protested Angela. 'I was hoping you'd stay for the night.'

'Not this time, thank you,' replied Win. 'Iseult has an appointment to keep and I promised Mark we would be back this evening.'

'But you'll have tea before you go. I insist,' said Angela, getting to her feet. 'I made scones specially. I'll go and put the kettle on.'

'We'll have to stay,' whispered Win when Angela had left the room.

'But we won't be there before six,' Iseult whispered back. 'I'll be too late.'

'We wouldn't be back before six if we left now,' replied Win. 'So you've decided you're going to marry him, have you?'

'Yes—I'll have to. I can't let Tim down ... at least I wasn't going to let him down if we could have got back before six,' Iseult muttered. 'Oh, what am I going to do now?'

'Go and see Nick as soon as you get back. Or go tomorrow. I'm sure he'll understand why you couldn't see him before six today when he knows you've been here with me,' replied Win comfortingly.

Stifling anxious thoughts about Tim, Iseult found she couldn't resist the Cornish tea of fresh home-made scones, thick clotted cream and fruit-bursting strawberry jam which Angela set before them. Again time seemed of no importance to Win or her friend, and it was well after seven when Win decided at last to leave.

Mist was drifting in from the sea again. Clammy and cold, it wreathed itself lazily among trees and across the roads and when they reached the high moors it thickened to shut out the views of the white pyramids of clay waste, often cutting down the speed of the car to a crawl. By the time they reached St Austell it was dark and as they drove down the river valley they met more fog, so that it was past ten when they eventually entered the gatehouse.

'Did Tim come to see Merlin this afternoon?'

Iseult asked Mark. He was in the studio working on some prints he was making.

'No. But I met him and Nick later, on the beach when I took the dog for a walk,' he replied, looking up at her. 'Nick gave me a message for you.'

'What is it?'

'He said I was to tell you they'll be leaving early in the morning to drive to Dorset, to visit a school there. He said you'd understand.'

'I see. Thanks.' She felt suddenly strangely chilly, as if she had been turned out of the house into the cold clammy mist. 'Angela bought the two pictures,' she said, in an effort to cheer herself up again. 'If they sell quickly she'll ask me for more.'

'Good for you.' He nodded and smiled at her in his usual vague way and turned his attention to the plate on which he was etching, and she guessed that as usual he was much more interested in his own artistic endeavours than he was in hers.

She went to bed, but not to sleep immediately. Lying listening to the owls hooting in the trees she thought of Tim again. How was he feeling? Was he lying awake too, miserable because Nicholas was going to carry out his threat and arrange for him to go to another boarding school just because she hadn't gone to Linyan House before six o'clock to say she would be Tim's stepmother?

As soon as it was light in the morning she would get up and go to the old house, hoping to arrive

there before they left for Dorset, and somehow
she would find a way to get through that hard
shell Nicholas had grown since Rosita had died.
Somehow she would prevent him from carrying
out his threat.

She set the alarm for seven and woke as soon as
it rang. Moving about quietly so as not to disturb
her parents, she washed and dressed, slipping into
thigh-moulding hip-hugging pants of silvery grey
which she topped with a loosely-knitted round-
necked sweater patterned in cable in two shades
of mauve. Over the sweater she pulled on a blazer-
styled jacket made from fine black and white
Donegal tweed. She brushed her mop of hair until
it glowed like a torch, made up her eyes and
outlined her lips with a dark red lipstick. Then,
satisfied that she looked her best, attractively
feminine in spite of the silver-grey pants, she
picked up her shoes and carrying them in one
hand tiptoed downstairs to the hall. There she
stopped to put on the shoes before stepping out
of the front door.

The morning air was cool and fresh and there
was no mist. Sunlight shafted down through the
branches of the trees where newly unfurled leaves
fluttered in a slight breeze. The driveway was
streaked with bars of yellow light and the dark
grey shadows of bushes and tree trunks. High
above in the pale blue sky fine feathers of clouds
drifted by. Birds whistled and sang in the bushes,
and although she couldn't see it from where she
was she could hear the sea singing too as it dashed

against rocks and sand.

She felt calm, her mind flooded with sunlight. It was as if she had come to the end of a particularly stormy and aggravating voyage and had arrived in harbour safely. She supposed she felt like that because she had made up her mind to marry Nicholas, even if she didn't like him.

Rounding the last bend in the driveway, she saw Linyan House glinting at her. Solidly built, it had withstood storms for almost two hundred years and it would probably withstand many more. The Veryans, too, had withstood many ups and downs, but the family had survived like the house.

Iseult was about to cross the lawn to the front door when the door opened and Nicholas came out. Closing the door behind him, he strode straight towards her, his tousled hair lifting in the breeze, his dark eyebrows slanting in a frown.

'Have you seen Tim?' he demanded when he was within speaking distance of her. He was casually dressed in dark pants and the same cream-coloured sweater he had worn when she had first met him, and he must have only just got up and left the house because he was unshaven, the blackness of his beard stubble making him look more than usually piratical. Surprised to see him, she felt the impact of his physical presence strike her like a blow to the heart. Her breath caught in her throat and her heart beat faster. In an attempt to cover up the sudden upheaval of her emotions she jammed her hands into the pockets of her tweed jacket, tossed back her head so that her hair shimmered in the sunlight and gave him a direct look, all her resolves to behave in a feminine way forgotten.

'No, I haven't,' she replied. 'Why should I have seen him?'

'I thought he might have gone running to the gatehouse for protection. Or to ask to be hidden from me, for a while,' he said, his mouth twisting unpleasantly. 'He knows we have to leave at eight-thirty if we want to reach the school at Brookhill by noon for the interview with the headmaster, and he doesn't want to go. I've been searching for him for half an hour. He wasn't in bed when I went to wake him at seven and he doesn't seem to be anywhere in the house or the outbuildings.' He slanted her a dark, hostile glance. 'Are you quite sure he isn't in the gatehouse?'

Keep your temper, keep your temper, Iseult warned herself. *Don't let his attitude get your goat.*

'He isn't there as far as I know,' she said quietly. 'But then I haven't looked for him. I've just come out.' She noticed for the first time how pale he was and how drawn about the eyes, as if he'd slept badly, and she felt sympathy stir within her. 'If you like you can come to the gatehouse and look for him,' she offered.

'Thanks.' He fell into step beside her and they walked in silence, but gradually she became aware of the force of the anger which was smouldering within him, beneath the outwardly cool manner, and she wondered how she could divert that anger from Tim before the boy was found.

'I was on my way to see you,' she said.

'Why?'

'To tell you I've decided to accept your proposal of marriage.'

'You're a little late, aren't you?' he replied jeeringly. 'It's almost fourteen hours past the deadline I set.'

'I know. But I couldn't come before six yesterday. I went to St Ives with Mother to deliver some of her pottery. We were late coming back, too late to come and tell you I'd made a decision.'

He stopped in mid-stride to swing round and look at her. For a moment they stood facing each other, like enemies eyeing each other before making the next move.

'I had one hell of a night with Tim because of you,' he grated between taut lips.

'I'm sorry, but it wasn't my fault,' she retorted. '*You* made the ultimatum and *you* fixed the deadline. If you hadn't you wouldn't have had anything to worry about when I didn't turn up in time.'

'If I hadn't you would never have made up your mind,' he countered mockingly. 'And that's one thing you've learned about me, darlin',' he continued. 'I'm a stickler for punctuality. When I said six o'clock Saturday evening I meant six o'clock Saturday evening and when you hadn't come by that time I assumed you'd decided against marriage to me. I told Tim and he burst into tears. He cried off and on most of the night.'

'I guessed he'd be upset and it worried me,' she confessed. 'That's why I came as early as I could this morning, and now that you know why I couldn't give you an answer yesterday surely you're willing to accept my answer now.'

He gave her an impatient exasperated glance and, turning away, began to stride down the driveway again.

'Oh, you must accept it, you must!' Iseult cried urgently, hurrying after him. 'I felt terrible when Dad gave me your message. You see, I didn't really believe you'd do what you threatened. I didn't believe you could be so ruthless.'

'Well, you know now,' Nicholas growled, striding on ahead of her.

'I had a bad night too,' she went on, annoyed because she was having to take running steps to keep up with him. 'I realised Tim was depending on me to accept your proposal, but I feel worse now that I know that rather than go with you to the school he's hidden.' She took a deep breath and added, 'You don't think he's run away, do you?'

To her relief he stopped and turned to her again. He was paler than ever and his eyes held a tormented expression. Sympathy swelled in her again. She wanted to go up to him, put a hand on his arm, comfort him in some way.

'He threatened to run away last night,' he replied. 'Let's go to the gatehouse,' he added gruffly, and taking hold of her elbow urged her to go with him along the driveway.

When they entered the kitchen at the gatehouse they were greeted by Merlin and the mouthwatering smell of the bacon and eggs Win was cooking.

'Mother, have you seen Tim?' Iseult lost no time in getting to the point. Win turned round and stared in surprise at her.

'I didn't know you were up and about,' she said, and her glance shifted to Nicholas. 'Is Tim missing?' she asked.

'I hope he's only hiding, hoping to delay our departure for Dorset until it's too late for us to go,' he replied. 'I'd like to find him to tell him we're not going after all.'

'Oh.' Win's shrewd glance slid to Iseult and back again to Iseult. Mark came into the kitchen. He was still in his pyjamas and was wearing an old woollen dressing gown over them.

'Good morning, Nick,' he said. 'I thought you were making an early start for Dorset.'

'He's not going,' said Win. 'Have you found someone to stay at Linyan and look after Tim, then?' she asked, turning back to Nicholas.

'I have.' A slight smile lightened the sombreness of his face. 'Iseult and I are going to be married. I hope neither of you object.'

'Even if we did object I imagine neither of you would pay any attention to our objection,' said Mark dryly. 'When and where?'

'Probably the day before I have to rejoin the ship. I can't see us being able to arrange it before then. We'd like you both to be there, at the Parish Church.'

from Tim before the boy was found.

'I was on my way to see you,' she said.

'Why?'

'To tell you I've decided to accept your proposal of marriage.'

'You're a little late, aren't you?' he replied jeeringly. 'It's almost fourteen hours past the deadline I set.'

'I know. But I couldn't come before six yesterday. I went to St Ives with Mother to deliver some of her pottery. We were late coming back, too late to come and tell you I'd made a decision.'

He stopped in mid-stride to swing round and look at her. For a moment they stood facing each other, like enemies eyeing each other before making the next move.

'I had one hell of a night with Tim because of you,' he grated between taut lips.

'I'm sorry, but it wasn't my fault,' she retorted. '*You* made the ultimatum and *you* fixed the deadline. If you hadn't you wouldn't have had anything to worry about when I didn't turn up in time.'

'If I hadn't you would never have made up your mind,' he countered mockingly. 'And that's one thing you've learned about me, darlin',' he continued. 'I'm a stickler for punctuality. When I said six o'clock Saturday evening I meant six o'clock Saturday evening and when you hadn't come by that time I assumed you'd decided against marriage to me. I told Tim and he burst into tears. He cried off and on most of the night.'

'I guessed he'd be upset and it worried me,' she confessed. 'That's why I came as early as I could this morning, and now that you know why I couldn't give you an answer yesterday surely you're willing to accept my answer now.'

He gave her an impatient exasperated glance and, turning away, began to stride down the drive-way again.

'Oh, you must accept it, you must!' Iseult cried urgently, hurrying after him. 'I felt terrible when Dad gave me your message. You see, I didn't really believe you'd do what you threatened. I didn't believe you could be so ruthless.'

'Well, you know now,' Nicholas growled, striding on ahead of her.

'I had a bad night too,' she went on, annoyed because she was having to take running steps to keep up with him. 'I realised Tim was depending on me to accept your proposal, but I feel worse now that I know that rather than go with you to the school he's hidden.' She took a deep breath and added, 'You don't think he's run away, do you?'

To her relief he stopped and turned to her again. He was paler than ever and his eyes held a tormented expression. Sympathy swelled in her again. She wanted to go up to him, put a hand on his arm, comfort him in some way.

'He threatened to run away last night,' he replied. 'Let's go to the gatehouse,' he added gruffly, and taking hold of her elbow urged her to go with him along the driveway.

feet, and he gave her a surprised glance. 'That is
. . . if you don't mind,' she added lamely.

'You can come if you want to,' he replied with
his usual casual indifference.

'And if Tim comes here you can be sure we'll
march him up to the house to account for himself
straight away,' said Win, going with them to the
door.

The sun was higher in the sky, shining straight
down on the driveway, so there were no more
streaks of yellow light. The air was soft and warm,
scented with newly turned earth and the tang of
the sea. It was a lovely morning in late spring and
if they had been marrying for love they would
have held hands, thought Iseult fancifully and
regretfully. Perhaps they would have stopped to
kiss occasionally. But they weren't in love with
each other. She glanced sideways at Nicholas.
Walking slowly, his head bent, he wasn't angry
any more, but he was withdrawn, indifferent to
her, as her mother had suggested he was, and his
attitude stung her, making her want to tantalize
him in some way to draw his attention to herself.

As soon as they entered the house Nicholas
called Tim's name and waited for an answer.
None came. He looked at Iseult and rubbed his
chin with his fingers.

'I'll go and shave,' he murmured. 'Make yourself at home. The study is always the best room
to be in this time of day, I think. It faces east
and south and gets all the morning sun. I won't

be long and then we'll talk. There are some legalities about our marriage we have to discuss.'

He went upstairs, and Iseult wandered through to the study. Sunlight glinted on the glass cases holding the models of various ships which Matthew Veryan had made with so much patience and care. It gave a golden sheen to the wood of the half models of ships which were attached to the walls and which he had also made. There were photographs too, scattered about the tops of the bookcases and on the mantelpiece over the hearth, mostly of ships, but some of their crews, and she found one of Nicholas, a younger Nicholas with blond-dark hair and a wide white grin. There were no photographs of women or of weddings in the room. But then women didn't stay long in this house, she was reminded, and the marriages didn't last long for one reason or another. Maybe she wouldn't stay long either and her marriage to Nicholas would last only as long as he wanted it to last.

Legalities to discuss. Iseult chewed at her lip. It sounded so cold, so unromantic. Pausing by the paper-littered desk, she looked down. Some letters, opened and read, then tossed aside, lay there. One on the top of the pile was written on pale blue deckle-edged paper which had an address embossed upon it under an important-looking heraldic crest. The writing, done in violet ink, was rounded and rather childish-looking. The signature at the bottom of the page was very clear, *Joanna*.

Joanna Trethowyn? Iseult stared at the letter. It wasn't long and she could read it quite quickly without picking it up. She read:

'Nick darling, I realise you are probably on the high seas, but I'm writing to you at Linyan anyway so that this will be waiting for you when you go home on leave. It was such fun seeing you in London in the autumn that I want to make sure we'll meet again soon.

'I'll be visiting Polruth in July and by then I hope to have some news which will please you. It seems ages since we were together. Remember how good it was? Be seeing you, Joanna.'

Hearing a noise coming from the hallway, Iseult moved quickly away from the desk and went over to the window seat. She looked through the window down the lawn to the gate in the wall, but she didn't really see anything that was there. Instead she was seeing in her mind's eye Pierre and Marie entwined on the bed on his studio. Pierre's hands were moving lustfully over Marie's bare, olive skin. Then Pierre changed, became a tall man with shaggy grey-dark hair, and Marie changed too, into a pretty white-skinned woman with long reddish-brown hair a red-lipped seductive smile and big, heavy-lidded slate blue eyes.

Iseult blinked and shook away the unpleasant fantasy, feeling as if she had just peeped into a particularly private part of Nicholas's life. She wasn't so naïve that she didn't know what Joanna meant by the phrases 'being together' and 'how good it was'. Nicholas and Joanna had been lovers ten years ago and had apparently been lovers since, even though both of them had been married to other people. She pressed a hand against her stomach. That awful sickness was clawing at her stomach as it had when she had walked in on Pierre and Marie.

She turned from the window, glanced once more at the letter, then crossed the room and hurried out into the hall, intending to leave. She couldn't marry Nicholas, not now, not after seeing that incriminating letter from Joanna. She couldn't promise to be his wife, live here at Linyan and wonder if he stayed with Joanna every time he visited London. Possibly that was what had happened to Rosita. Well, it wasn't going to happen to her. She would leave now and send him a note telling him she had changed her mind about marrying him.

She was turning the knob on the front door when she heard the noise she had heard before, a thumping sound which she had thought had been Nicholas's footsteps as he had come downstairs but which she now realised was coming from behind one of the wooden panels in the hallway. It sounded as if someone was kicking the panel from the other side.

Tim! Tim had found the secret door, opened it and gone down to the cellar to hide until it was too late to go to Dorset. Hurriedly she went over to the panel from which the sound was coming and leaned her head against it. The thumping began again and faintly, very faintly through the thick wood, she heard a voice calling, although she couldn't make out what it was saying.

With both hands she searched the panelling for the button that would release the spring lock and open the door. It was no use. She couldn't find it and couldn't even guess in which of the many curved roses it was situated. She would have to go upstairs and ask Nicholas to come down and open the door to let Tim out instead of rushing out of the house to go as far away from Linyan as possible.

She walked upstairs to the landing above and looked round wondering where the bathroom was.

'Nicholas? Where are you?' she called hesitantly.

'Here.' His voice came from an open doorway on the left. She went over to the doorway, pushed the door open farther and stepped into a big bedroom furnished with a wide bed which had old-fashioned mahogany bed ends, a huge mahogany dressing table and a massive wardrobe made from the same wood which seemed to take up the whole of one wall. An Indian carpet patterned in red and gold covered the floor and the curtains which hung at the two windows were made from gold-coloured velvet. Depressingly dark wallpaper decorated in a rose pattern of red flock on a gold background covered the walls.

Nicholas was standing in front of one of the open doors of the wardrobe. Dressed only in brief underpants, he was taking a pair of trousers from a hanger. Iseult watched the muscles of his shoulders shift sinuously beneath the sheath of his suntanned skin as he put the hanger back in the wardrobe and closed the door. He turned, saw her staring at him and stared back, one eyebrow going up enquiringly.

'What's the matter?' he asked, his mouth quirking with humour. 'Don't tell me you've never seen a man undressed before and are shocked. Do you know you're as white as a sheet?' He frowned, his eyes narrowing. 'No, more than that. You look green as if you're going to be sick. Are you sure you're all right?'

Tossing the trousers down on the bed, he came round towards her, lean and mostly bare, a sinewy broad-shouldered man with a narrow waist, slim hips and long well-shaped legs, who moved with an animal-like grace. She would have backed out of the doorway, but she misjudged where she was and backed into the wall beside the door. Nicholas stopped before her, hands on his hips to lean forward slightly and study her face more closely. She felt herself shrinking back against the wall.

'I'd like to know what that Frenchman did to you to make you so damned nervous of men,' he said softly, his dark eyes seeming to pierce hers so that she looked away from his eyes to his mouth, watching the broadly-moulded lips curl back from his teeth as he spoke. The scents of his skin and hair were tantalising her nose and she began to breathe hard, almost panting in her fear. 'I'd like to touch you, stroke your cheek, run my fingers through that mop of hair, kiss you,' he went on, his voice still soft, 'but I'm sure you'd push me away if I did and run from the house. And I don't want you to run away now that you've said you'll marry me. Why did you come up here? What do you want?'

'It ... it's Tim. I think he's in the cellar, or at least behind the secret door.' Now she couldn't tear her glance away from his mouth as she wondered what it would be like to be kissed by him. 'I can hear some banging come from behind a panel in the hallway,' she muttered. 'I would have opened it, but I don't know where the button is that releases the spring.'

'The little devil!' His lips curved back in a snarl, but in the next instant were twitching with amusement. 'I should have guessed where he was hiding. He's been fascinated by that door and has been trying to find it ever since we came here.' He turned away from her and she sagged with relief against the wall, watching him step into the trousers and pull them up. When they were fastened he turned towards the door again, frowning, anger smouldering beneath the surface again.

'Please don't be angry with him,' Iseult said urgently as she followed him along the landing to the stairs, but he ignored her and ran barefooted down the stairs. By the time she caught up with him the secret door was sliding back to reveal Tim, his pale face streaked with dirt, his dark eyes panic-stricken. As soon as he saw Nicholas he lunged forward and clasped him about the hips.

'I did it to frighten you,' he sobbed. 'I was going to stay down there until it was too late to go, but I got frightened instead. It's horrid down there, so I came up, and I couldn't open the door.' He broke off, took a long shaky breath and pushing away from Nicholas, glared up at him, rebellion showing in the thrust of his lower lip. 'But I'm not going to that school. I won't go. I won't go!'

'All right,' replied Nicholas coolly. 'You don't have to go.'

'But you said. . . .'

'Look around you, Tim, see who's here.'

Tim looked round and saw Iseult. His black eyes widened lit up and he smiled.

'Hello, Isa,' he said. 'Why didn't you come yesterday?'

'Hello, Tim. I couldn't come because I went out with my mother. I came this morning instead.'

'And are you. . . .' Tim broke off again, to glance warily at Nicholas, then he looked at her again. 'Are you and him——' he went on ungrammatically.

'He,' Nicholas corrected him.

'Are you going to be married to each other?' Tim asked hopefully, still looking at Iseult.

She thought ruefully of her earlier intention to run from the house and to send Nicholas a note telling him she had changed her mind about marrying him. She thought of the deckle-edged blue notepaper covered with Joanna's handwriting. She looked into Tim's hopeful black eyes and knew that the opportunity to change her mind was lost. She was committed now for better or for worse.

'Yes,' she said, smiling at him. 'We're going to be married to each other.'

CHAPTER FIVE

SEVERAL times during the next two weeks Iseult thought of running away, of escaping from the commitment she had made, but always the thought of what would happen to Tim held her back. She saw him and Nicholas at least once every day, sometimes at the gatehouse and sometimes at Linyan House.

Two days before the marriage ceremony was to take place Nicholas drove her into St Austell to visit the firm of lawyers who had always looked after the affairs of the Veryan family and they signed a contract which Nicholas had had drawn up which gave her the right to act as Tim's legal guardian during his father's absence.

It was on the return trip to Polruth that she was able at last to ask a question which had been hovering on the tip of her tongue for a few days but which, for some reason, she had not been able to ask.

'How long?' she asked abruptly.

'You might fill me in,' he replied, mocking her as usual. 'What is how long?'

'How long do you want the arrangement ... our marriage to last?'

'A marriage is supposed to be a "till death us do part" affair,' he said dryly.

'But this marriage is different. We're marrying for Tim's sake and not because we want to live together,' she argued, turning to him. Against the sunlight shafting through the car window beside him his profile was dark and stern, as remote as ever. Even after meeting him and talking with him every day for almost two weeks she felt she didn't know him any better than she had before. He kept his distance. But then she supposed she kept distant from him too. 'One day Tim will be able to look after himself,' she added. 'By the time he's in his teens he'll be able to cope with boarding school.'

'That's true,' he conceded. 'But by then there'll be other children, *our* children, and they'll need the care of a mother no less than Tim does now.'

There was a tense uneasy silence. Iseult looked away out of the window beside her at the green curves of the river valley and the shining ribbon of water. Her stomach was turning over as it always did when she thought of the physical side of their forthcoming marriage. How on earth was she going to go through with it? How would she be able to bear the touch of his hands and lips, knowing that he didn't love her and that she didn't love him?

'I'd like you to have the use of the car while I'm away.' His voice cut across her woolly, confused thoughts. 'After the marriage ceremony we'll drive towards Southampton. I'll make a reservation for us to stay at a hotel, possibly in Bournemouth. Next morning I'll go by bus to the docks at Southampton to join the ship and you can drive back to Linyan. Do you think you can manage the long drive on your own?'

'Won't we be taking Tim with us?' she asked.

'No. It isn't usual to take a child on a honeymoon,' Nicholas replied coolly. 'Win says he can stay with her and Mark until you get back.'

'But....' She broke off, confused again, and caught her lower lip between her teeth. 'I don't think our sort of marriage merits a honeymoon,' she muttered.

'What the hell do you mean by "our sort of marriage"?' he said acidly. 'Just because we're marrying in a hurry to provide Tim with another legal guardian while I'm away at sea it doesn't make it any less of a marriage to my way of thinking.' He paused, then continued, 'You were hoping I'd go away without consummating it, weren't you?'

'Yes,' she muttered truthfully.

'Yet I've warned you that it isn't going to be a marriage on paper only,' he replied. 'A business arrangement, yes, an equal partnership with you putting as much into the relationship as I am, so don't think for one moment you're getting a free ride. Do I make myself clear?'

'Very clear,' she retorted. As usual he had managed to rouse her pride. Apathy was banished and she hated him fiercely for his blunt speaking. 'But don't expect me to enjoy the honeymoon.' She spoke between her teeth, and could have hit him when all he did was laugh at her.

But for all her occasional outbursts of irritation with him she made no attempt to stop the course of events. She was like a leaf which had been caught in a strong current and was being swept downstream towards a meeting with the restless overwhelming sea. She was on a journey she had never intended to make but on which she had to continue for Tim's sake.

For Tim's sake she went through the marriage ceremony one morning in Polruth Parish Church where so many Veryans had been baptised, married and buried over hundreds of years and where some of them were remembered on the stone walls for having endowed the church in the past. For Tim's sake she spoke the vows set down in the prayer book. For Tim's sake she allowed Nicholas to push a ring on her finger and then to kiss her briefly on the mouth. For Tim's sake she stepped into the blue car and let herself be driven away on the final part of the journey, across the Tamar River, the natural border dividing Cornwall from the rest of England, through the rolling Devonshire countryside, laced by dark foliage and green fields mottled with cattle and sheep.

On through rural Dorset Nicholas drove, not turning off to take the road to the seaside resort of Bournemouth as she had expected but continuing on into Hampshire to follow a twisting road which dipped up and down under drooping branches of old trees to a village of houses with thatched roofs, where he stopped the car in front of a gabled coaching inn.

In the low-beamed dining room where antique brass gleamed against oak darkened with age they dined on duckling garnished with orange sauce, fruit pie with thick fresh cream and a light white wine.

'I thought we were going to stay the night in Bournemouth,' said Iseult.

'I decided this would be quieter and more suited to our needs,' he replied. 'Also there are no locks on the bedroom door.'

Across the table, above the candle flame, his dark eyes challenged her. Maybe it was because of the wine he had drunk that he seemed more relaxed than she had ever known him to be since she had met him. The line of his mouth had softened and there was an upward tilt to one corner of his lips as if he were about to smile at her. No longer was he the captain in command of a ship, issuing orders and expecting them to be obeyed. He was a man at his ease, looking for entertainment and possibly hoping to find it in her.

Iseult's nerves quivered as she thought of the

bedroom upstairs with its double four-poster bed and its pretty latticed windows. It had no lock on its door. She couldn't lock Nicholas out any more. They were married and according to the ancient custom he had the right to sleep with her whenever he wished.

Her hand shook and wine slopped over the edge of the glass as she set it down. She dabbed at her lips with the white damask table napkin and placed it beside her empty plate. Finding her handbag, she slung it over her shoulder and stood up, tall and slim in her lilac-coloured suit, her hair competing with the candle-flame in colour and brightness.

'Going somewhere?' Nicholas asked smoothly, rising to his feet.

'For a walk,' she muttered. 'It was a long drive and I feel the need for exercise.'

There was no escaping him. As she crossed the room and went out into the entrance hall he was with her, opening the front door of the inn for her, stepping out beside her into the village street.

They walked in silver for the sun had set, white mist was rising from the river meadows and a full moon shone. Down a silver lane, past silver trees and a silver barn to a silver bridge spanning the silver stream. On the bridge they stopped to look down at the silver-spangled water and to listen to its tinkling music.

'Perhaps we'll see the ghost,' murmured Nicholas.

'What ghost?' Iseult turned to him and found him close, too close for comfort, so she side-stepped away from him.

'The woman in the crinoline dress who's supposed to have thrown herself off the bridge when she discovered her lover was unfaithful to her,' he replied, mockery edging his voice. 'What foolish things women do for love,' he added softly.

'Don't you mean for lack of love?' she countered. 'She drowned herself because he didn't love her. But I agree with you, she was foolish, to throw away her life just because she'd discovered the truth about him.'

'And you would never even consider doing anything like that?' he probed quietly, shifting until he was close to her again, his shoulder nudging hers as they leaned together on the stone wall of the bridge.

'No. Never.' Iseult moved back from the wall, away from him again, and began to walk back over the bridge, the way they had come.

He didn't walk with her and by the time she had reached the inn he hadn't caught up with her. She went through the dimly lit quiet entrance hall and up the staircase to the bedroom. Perhaps if she went to bed now she would be asleep by the time he came, and even if she weren't she could pretend to be asleep and so avoid his intention to consummate their marriage tonight.

But he must have been right behind her when she had entered the inn, for she was still in the process of undressing, had sat down on the edge of the bed to roll down her nylon tights when the door opened without ceremony.

Closing the door behind him, Nicholas leaned against it. In the lamplight the collar of his white shirt gleamed emphasizing the tan of his face. Beneath the level black eyebrows his eyes were pools of darkness, their glance directed to the slim white shapeliness of her legs as she withdrew the flimsy pale nylon from her feet. His presence in the room seemed to freeze her nerves. Her tights bunched in one hand, she sat as if petrified, dressed only in the lilac-coloured silky lace-edged slip she had worn under her suit and blouse.

'Don't let me stop you from taking the rest off,' he drawled, lunging away from the door, his hand at the knot of his tie, loosening it. Still unable to move, her heart knocking against her ribs, her throat dry with panic, Iseult hardly heard the rustle of clothing as he undressed, was not aware of him until suddenly the bed beside her sank down as he sat on it and she saw his thigh, thick and muscular, the skin sprinkled with dark hairs, close to her rounded white one. His hand reached across in front of her and the nerves in her stomach contracted—but he was only reaching for her tights, to take them from her hand and toss them aside.

There was a short pause in which neither of them spoke nor moved. Iseult could hear the steady thud of his heart and her own heart's swift, tripping panic beat. She could feel the heat of his bare body and longed suddenly to warm her own coolness against that heat. But she couldn't move. She was like a wild, shy animal frozen to immobility when at last it is cornered by the predatory beast which has been stalking it.

Then she felt his fingers move lightly on her skin, sliding beneath the strap of her slip, lifting it up and over the curve of her shoulder, slipping it down her arm, and she shivered uncontrollably. Nicholas's hand left the strap, lifted to her chin, forcing her face up so he could see it, but she refused to look at him, kept her eyelids down, the dark sweep of her eyelashes covering her eyes.

'Iseult, look at me.'

'No, no, I can't, I don't want to.' Her voice came out in a groaning whisper. 'I don't want to!'

His answer was swift, taking her by surprise. Hard and demanding, his lips covered hers in a ruthless kiss from which there was no escape and his heavy shoulders pushing against hers forced her backwards until she felt the softness of the old-fashioned candlewick bedspread against her skin. She came to life then, breaking out of the frozen condition, trying to wrench her mouth free of his, hitting at him with clenched but futile fists.

At last he lifted his head and looked down at her, but he didn't move away and she was still trapped by the pressure of his legs against hers.

'Now, are you going to stop pretending?' he asked softly.

He was a different person, a satyr with slanting

dark eyebrows, glittering lustful eyes and a sensually curved mouth whose bare skin had a golden sheen in the lamplight, tempting her fingers to touch his shoulders and slide over his back.

'Pretending what?' she whispered.

'Pretending that you don't know how and that you don't want to. Pretending that this has never happened to you before and that you've never been kissed like I've just kissed you or that you've never been touched like this.' His hand swept insolently over the breast he had bared and her nerves leapt in response, tingling deliciously throughout her whole body. 'You had a lover in Paris, remember,' he continued tauntingly, and bent his head to lick the vulnerable hollow at the pulse of the throat, and again she felt those insidious tingles run riot along her nerves. 'You were going to marry him,' he murmured, raising a hand to stroke her cheek, his fingers drifting upwards to slide seductively over the delicate skin at her temple before thrusting greedily into her hair. 'Or so you told your mother,' he added suggestively, 'so that she wouldn't worry about you, so that she wouldn't think you were having an illicit relationship with him.'

'I told her that because I believed Pierre when he said he wanted to marry him and for no other reason,' she protested.

'You believed him and he seized the opportunity of having you trust him to make love to you,' he retorted.

'But we didn't ... I mean, I wouldn't go all the

way before we were married.' She saw scepticism gleam in his eyes and twist his mouth and suddenly realised what he was implying; he was implying that she wasn't a virgin. 'Oh, please believe me. I wouldn't go all the way before marriage. I couldn't,' she insisted breathlessly.

'You can now because you're married to me,' Nicholas mocked softly, but there was a strange blaze in his eyes as his face came closer to hers again. 'You can go all the way with me, my reluctant bride.'

There was no escape. His lips dominated hers again and the strong current which had borne her so surely to that moment in time met the wild floodtide of his passion. Swamped by new and exciting physical sensations that made her mind reel, she was drawn unresistingly into and gradually engulfed by a whirlpool of sensual pleasure from which she surfaced later, feeling lighter than a feather, to float on gentle swaying waves, her head pillowed on something firm and warm which she had wetted with tears of pain and exaltation.

The knocking on the door was loud. It was repeated and was followed by a voice which spoke in a thick Hampshire burr.

'Mrs Veryan, I've brought your tea. Shall I bring it in?'

Startled, Iseult lunged up in bed, the sheet falling away from her exposing her nakedness. All the other bedclothes seemed to have disappeared. Looking over the edge of the bed, she saw they

were in a heap on the floor. As memories of all
that had happened the previous night crowded
into her mind her cheeks burned suddenly with
hot blood. Hunching the the sheet about her, she
called,

'Yes, yes, please, come in.'

The latch lifted on the door and a small plump
woman who was wearing an apron over her blouse
and skirt entered. She greeted Iseult with a pleasant good morning and slid a tray on to the bedside
table. On the tray was a teapot, nestled into a
padded linen cosy, and a china cup and saucer.

'Mr Veryan ordered it for you before he left,'
said the woman, twitching back the curtains to let
more light into the room. Raindrops spattered
against the pane.

'What time is it?' asked Iseult. She could not
help feeling a little hurt because Nicholas had left
without waking her to say goodbye.

'Half past eight. Your hubby caught the eight-
fifteen train from the junction. He says you'll be
driving back to Cornwall by yourself. You'd like
breakfast before you go, I expect.'

'Yes, please.'

The woman went out and, sitting up in bed
again, Iseult lifted the tea-cosy. The tea had been
brewed in a sculptured silver teapot and there was
a matching strainer. On a small plate there were
three shortbread biscuits. Beside the plate was a
spray of azalea blossoms, their pinkish purple
petals still sprinkled with raindrops. They had
obviously been picked recently from a bush in the

garden of the old inn.

Picking up the azaleas, she found an envelope under them with her name written on it. Excitement beat through her, tautening her limbs and breasts, chasing away the delicious languor she had been feeling, almost as if Nicholas had come into the room and had touched her.

Putting down the azaleas, she poured tea with a hand which shook slightly, put the cosy back on the pot, picked up the envelope and leaned back against the pillows to study Nicholas's handwriting. It was dark and bold, like him, she thought fancifully.

Last night, like his pirate forebears, he had taken what he had wanted in a wild tumultuous mating with her. But he had given, too, drawing from her with subtle tender caresses a response she would never have believed she was capable of achieving. His touch had released something in her, a hidden spring like that which opened the secret door at Linyan House, opening her heart and her body to his invasion so that shyly and inexpertly, it was true, she had followed his lead, touching and caressing him. She could never say he had taken what he had wanted from her against her will or without giving her something in return.

Slowly she slid the single piece of paper from the envelope, opened it and read.

'I am not going to ask you to forgive me for what happened last night,' he had written. 'I could excuse myself by saying that it might not

have happened so violently if you could have
trusted me enough to have confided the truth
about your affair with the Frenchman sooner. By
the time you told me I was fast losing control,
and can only say now you went to my head more
than any wine ever does.

'Drive carefully on your way back to Linyan.
I'll see you in about six weeks' time. I stole the
azalea flowers from the garden here. They're for
you. Give my love to Tim. Nick.'

The tea in the cup went cold as Iseult read and
re-read the note. He sent his love to Tim, but
there was no word of love for her. Yet he had
stolen the azalea blossoms from the garden for
her. Smiling a little, she picked up the flowers
and touched her lips to them. She felt different,
sure of herself in a way she had never felt before,
and all because the man whom she had married
so that she could look after his son had admitted
she had gone to his head and had sent her flowers
he had taken from a garden.

It was surprising how quickly and easily she
settled into Linyan House with Tim and after a
week or so she began to feel she had lived there
all her life. It was surprising too how quickly she
became accustomed to being called Mrs Veryan
by various people in the town. Changing her name
was something she had once vowed she would
never do if she ever married. Now she accepted
the Veryan name with a certain amount of pride,
discovering that as the mistress of the 'Captain's

House' she commanded respect and acknow-
ledgement which had not been shown to her
before.

And as the weeks went by and she was occupied
with keeping house, attending to Tim as well as
painting more pictures and helping Win in the
small gallery in Polruth now that tourists were
beginning to appear in the district, the affair with
Pierre was almost forgotten. The wound he had
inflicted upon her sensibilities seemed to have
been cauterised by the one night of passion she
had spent with Nicholas, and it was healing fast.

With June better weather came. Roses bloomed
in the garden at Linyan, their scent heavy at the
end of the day when long windless twilights pre-
vailed. And often before dusk fell Iseult heard the
nightjar call its low churring, compelling cry,
primitive and insistent. There was no sweetness
in it, no nightingale romanticism, but it stirred
her blood, quickened her pulse and she thought
of Nicholas and what being with him again would
be like when he returned home.

One Saturday, at Tim's request she rented the
same day boat in which she had sailed with him
and Nicholas and the two of them floated across
the bay to Potter's Pyll, the water chuckling under
the bow. Once again they anchored and went
ashore in the tiny dinghy to eat their lunch.

After eating they walked along the path to the
headland and looked out to sea. In the sun-shim-
mered distance an oil tanker made a long dark
shape on the mist-blue water.

'I wish it was Dad's,' said Tim with a sigh. 'I wish he'd come home soon.'

Iseult glanced at him sharply. It was the first time since Nicholas had gone back to sea that the boy had mentioned him.

'I hadn't realised you miss him so much,' she said gently, shading her eyes against the sun's rays so as to see the ship better. It was going away from them, down Channel towards the Atlantic.

'Don't you?' Tim replied.

Did she? Lowering her hand, she looked around her, at the green grass starred with daisies and buttercups, over the edge of the cliff at the dark rocky shore of Marriott's Cove where Nicholas had first suggested that she marry him, and then back at the smudged shape of the ship which was hull down now and almost gone. Where was Nicholas now? Was he on the bridge deck of a similar ship as it ploughed up and down the waves of another sea? Or was he sleeping in his cabin? Perhaps he was supervising the docking procedure in some far-off and exotic port in the Middle East. Or perhaps he was ashore in such a port, enjoying himself. Wherever he was did he ever think of her and wonder what she was doing? Or wasn't that part of their arrangement?

'Don't you miss him?' Tim persisted.

'Yes, yes, I do,' she answered quickly. 'Do you want to walk any farther, go down on the beach in the cove and walk along to the caves?' she asked.

He walked to the edge of the cliff and looked

down the path, then stepped back quickly and said in a whispered,

'There's someone coming—a man. Do you think we're trespassing?'

'We might be. I'm not sure whether this land is private or not.'

'Let's go back to the dinghy,' he urged, coming over to her and pulling at her hand.

'All right.' She turned with him and they began to walk along the path back to the shore at Potter's Pyll.

'Hi there!' The voice behind them was slightly breathless and they both turned to face the man who was striding along after them. 'I saw you when I was on the beach in the cove,' he said. 'Did you come in that boat?' He jerked his head in the direction of the moored dayboat which was sidling round, as the tide turned, to point its bow towards the entrance to the pool, as if eager to be on its way.

'Yes,' replied Iseult warily. 'We sailed over from Polruth.'

'Just the two of you?'

'That's right.'

'Intrepid mariners,' he remarked, his mouth widening into a smile. He was of medium height, not much taller than herself, slightly built, and there was something familiar about him. His hair was curly and rather long, light brown in colour and his wide-set eyes were bluish grey. He was wearing jeans and a brightly patterned shirt which had not been made in England but looked

Hawaiian in design. A gold medallion hanging from the thin gold chain glinted against his chest within the opening of the shirt.

'I'm Charles Marriott,' he said, holding out his hand, 'and I have a feeling I should know you. You're not unlike a fair chap I used to know and who lived near Polruth, Tristram Severn.'

'I'm his sister Iseult,' she replied, smiling back at him and shaking his hand, her wariness gone. He had been a friend of her brother's and that was sufficient recommendation for her. 'I thought I recognised you, but couldn't be sure.'

'Iseult the Fair,' he murmured, holding her hand slightly longer than necessary while his blue-grey glance lingered on her hair and then on her face. 'Well, I'm glad I walked over to speak to you.' His glance slid down towards Tim who was staring at him belligerently, his black eyebrows slanting in a ferocious frown that made him look for a fleeting moment like Nicholas. 'And you're Tim, my umpteenth cousin several times removed,' Charles said with a grin. 'Do you remember me?'

Tim shook his head negatively and managed to look even more belligerent.

'Isa is married to my dad,' he announced gruffly.

There was no doubt that Charles Marriott was surprised. His eyes widened and he stared at her.

'Really?' he asked.

'Really,' she replied.

'Since when?'

'Since the twenty-fourth of May.'

'Only a month ago?' he exclaimed. 'And since I returned to this country. What a pity I didn't know. I'd have come down sooner and danced at your wedding. Is Nick at Linyan?'

'No. He's at sea, but he'll be back in about two weeks' time. Are you staying long?'

'All summer and maybe longer. It all depends on how the writing goes, whether inspiration lasts. After five years of script-writing in Hollywood I've come back to write my masterpiece, I hope.' His grin was attractively self-mocking. 'A play for the live theatre. Where's Tris these days?'

She began to tell him, but was interrupted by Tim, who took hold of one of her hands possessively and began to pull as if to urge her towards the dinghy.

'Come on, Isa,' he ordered. 'The tide has turned and it's time we started to sail back to the harbour. It'll take us hours, because there isn't much wind.'

'All right, young'un, I can take a hint. You don't like having me around, so I'll be on my way, back to my typewriter.' Charles looked across at Iseult. 'I'll call to see you one day, when I'm over the other side. Okay with you?'

'Yes, of course. We'll be pleased to see you,' she replied.

She had almost forgotten that Charles had said he would call and was surprised one afternoon when he arrived in a small sports car. She was on the lawn, painting a quick impression of the house with acrylic paint on a canvas, and he came across the grass to stand beside her and study the painting on the easel.

'I'd have come to see you before this, but the muse has been with me,' he drawled. 'My meeting with you at Potter's Pyll must have inspired me. How long have you been painting?'

'Ever since my father put a paintbrush in my hand and showed me how to use paint. I used to copy everything he did.'

'You're good,' he said admiringly.

'But not as good as he is, and I'm fast coming to the conclusion I'll never be as good. I don't possess his imagination. I've mastered the skill of how to put paint on canvas or paper and I can create pretty pictures, that's all. I call them "crowd-pleasers",' she said with a touch of self-mockery.

'So what's wrong with that?' he replied. 'I've been doing it for the past five years too, writing scripts for T.V. series strictly designed to entertain and please the crowds who watch. The masses, the people in the street are the ones you should aim to please, in my opinion. I like your painting. It makes me feel good to look at it, assures me that there's still a lot of beauty in this world if you only know how to look for it. To hell with the critics who say a painter or a writer has to shock or show the ugly side of life before he or she can be accounted as a true artist.'

'Well, thank you. I'm glad you came. You've

made my day,' Iseult replied lightly, smiling at him.

'You're very different from Rosita,' he said, his glance going over her untidy hair, her paint-flecked shirt and jeans, down to her bare feet.

'Did you know her?' She was surprised.

'For a short time, yes. She was here when I was staying at the Cove a few years ago, before I went to the States.'

'As different from her as chalk is from cheese?' she asked mockingly, as she swirled her brush in water to clean it and then wiped it on a rag.

'Now you're insulting me,' he retorted. 'Never would I use such a hackneyed cliché.' Again his glance roved over her assessingly. 'I would put it this way. You're as different from Rosita as a wild English daffodil is from an exotic South American orchid.'

'Mmm.' A slight smile flickered about Iseult's mouth as she squeezed paint from a tube on to her palette. 'I know my hair is yellow, but I'm not sure I like being described as wild.'

'By wild I meant natural, the sort of daffodil that grows "Beside the lake, beneath the trees", as Wordsworth put it. Not cultivated or forced in any way, sturdy and able to withstand the buffets of the British weather. Not brought up in a hot-house climate like Rosita was and therefore not so likely to wilt when brought to live in an old draughty house on the Cornish coast.'

'Oh, Linyan House isn't that bad,' Iseult replied as she stroked burnt sienna paint with her brush on to the canvas. 'I like living in it. It has character.'

'But you understand it and know its history. You know about the Veryans too, and how unpredictable they can be. Rosita came here from a totally different environment, from the warmth and gaiety of Rio.' He paused, frowning, then added, 'Nick should never have brought her here, nor left her here.' He gave her a quick wary glance. 'Sorry, Iseult—I suppose I shouldn't be discussing Nick's previous wife with you.'

'It's all right. I don't resent her. In fact I'd like to know more about her. Nick has never talked about her to me and all Tim remembers is that she used to hug him and cry a lot.' She stood back to survey the picture. 'That will do for now. I can finish it later. Would you like to come in the house and have a beer? Nick left some in the larder.'

They sat in the study, on the window seat, and sipped the beer from old pewter tankards.

'The house seems lighter somehow.' Charles remarked.

'Nick is redecorating it gradually. When he was home last he did the hallway and landing. I think he did this room when he was home before that.'

'Had you been going with him long, before you were married, I mean?' Charles asked.

'No.' She looked at him. Although there was a certain weakness in his face about the mouth and chin, there was kindness too, and she decided to trust him. 'We didn't marry for love but for Tim's sake. He was unhappy at boarding school. Nicholas thought he would be better living here with someone to look after him. It's a convenient arrangement for all of us.'

'You're very honest,' he remarked. 'Most women would never admit they hadn't been married for love. That was Rosita's trouble. Because Nick had rescued her from some dreadful, worse-than-death situation in Rio she believed he was in love with her and that he should be with her all the time, sheltering her and protecting her.' He drank some beer, leaned back and looked around the room. 'It must be nearly four years since I was last in this room, summoned here by Uncle Matthew. It was the beginning of October, I remember, and we'd had some terrible weather, storms followed by thick fogs. He wanted to know if I knew Rosita had gone. She'd been missing for a week before he made any move. He didn't like her, you know. He thought she wasn't good enough for Nick and had trapped Nick into marrying her.'

'Why would he think you knew where she'd gone?'

'Someone had told him she was having an affair with me while Nick was away at sea.'

'Was she?'

'No.' Charles shook his head from side to side. 'She was very lovely and I felt sorry for her and I could understand why Nick had married her. She had the ability to arouse the protective instincts in a man. She used to come over to the cottage at the cove and we'd talk, just like you and I are talking now. She'd tell me how she hated this place, how Uncle Matthew hated her, how much she missed Nick and how she longed to go back to Rio. The last time I saw her she told me that she thinking of leaving and going back to Brazil while he was away, so that she wouldn't be there when he came home on leave and maybe that would prove to him once and for all that she couldn't do what he wanted. She couldn't live here so that his son could grow up in England unless he lived with her all the time.' Charles tipped the tankard to his lips and drained it. 'But that's as far as my friendship with her went. I didn't ask her to go away with me to the States, yet someone told Matthew that I had.'

'Did you know who the someone was?'

'I didn't know for sure, but I could guess. If I tell you my guess, will you keep it to yourself?'

'Of course.'

'Did you ever meet Joanna Trethowyn?'

'Many times when I was a girl. She used to go about with Tris.'

'Until Nick came on the scene,' said Charles with a wry grin. 'I remember that. Joanna made a beeline for Nick as soon as he came home on leave that summer.' He laughed and shook his head incredulously. 'He always had a *je ne sais quoi* about him that attracted women who were looking for a strong, silent enigmatical hero who would solve all their problems, besides giving them status and security. Joanna came from a poor family and she always had an ambition to marry into the wealthiest family around here, the Veryans, and to be the mistress of the Captain's House. God knows she tried hard enough to get Nick to propose to her that summer.'

'I didn't know she was here at the time Rosita lived at Linyan,' said Iseult, fascinated in spite of herself in his commentary on events which had happened long ago.

'She came back to bury her grandmother. She was married by then to a wealthy stockbroker and lived in London. Nick introduced her to Rosita and they became quite friendly. You must have seen them together, walking through the woods on the beach.'

'No. I wasn't here then. I was away, studying at an art college in the north of England. But why would Joanna tell Nick's father that you and Rosita were having an affair?'

'I don't know, and I was never able to confront her with my suspicion because she left Polruth to return to London the same day Rosita left Linyan House. Then I went to the States and forgot all about the matter until I received a letter from my mother saying that Rosita's body had been found washed up on the beach at Marriott's Cove after a particularly bad storm. That was a shock, I can tell you.' Charles sighed and rose to his feet and put the empty tankard down on the desk. 'Poor little Rosita,' he murmured. 'I don't suppose we'll ever know if she drowned herself deliberately or whether it was an accident.'

Iseult felt cold suddenly, remembering the story Nick had told her about the woman who had drowned herself because she had discovered her lover had been unfaithful to her.

'Why would she have drowned herself deliberately?' she asked.

'Again, I'm only guessing,' Charles cautioned her, swinging round to face her, leaning his hips against the desk. 'I believe Rosita's unhappiness was caused by something more fundamental than having to live here at Linyan without Nick. I believe she'd discovered that her knight in shining armour was involved with another woman, that he had, in fact, a mistress. And she couldn't take it.'

'What other woman?' Iseult demanded. She was feeling colder than ever and wishing now that she hadn't let him continue to discuss Nicholas's previous wife.

'Can't you guess?' he said, leaning towards her, his blue-grey eyes bright with malice.

'Not ... not ... Joanna.' Her glance went past him to the desk. No opened letters were scattered carelessly on it yet she could imagine the letter from Joanna that she had read was still there, with its sickening, insinuating message.

'Who else?' he replied dryly.

'But you said Nick introduced Joanna to Rosita,' she argued. 'Surely he wouldn't do that if he was involved with her?'

'He couldn't avoid introducing them. When Joanna arrived in Polruth the first place she visited was this house on hearing that Nick was home and had his wife with him. And you can be sure she would be quick to let Rosita know that Nick had been her friend first, before he ever went to Rio and got himself a wife.' Charles lunged away from the desk and paced up and down the room, hands in the pockets of his jeans. 'Can't you hear her?' he said dramatically. 'Can't you imagine what hints she'd let drop in the course of conversation with Rosita as they walked along the beach out there?' He turned and looked across the desk at Iseult. 'No one who was as insecure as Rosita was could put up with those sort of insinuations for long without cracking and without jumping to the conclusion that Nick and Joanna had had a very close relationship and were still very close,' he added.

'All she had to do was ask Nick about it when he came home on leave,' said Iseult coolly.

'Maybe she was afraid to ask him because she knew what the answer would be,' he retorted. 'By the way, when do you expect him home?'

'On Tuesday next.'

'Good. I'll come over to see him, if I may. Right now I'd best be leaving and getting back to the typewriter. It's been nice talking to you, Iseult.'

She followed him to the front door and out on to the drive. Tim was standing by the sports car examining it.

'Is this yours?' he asked Charles.

'Sure is. Like to come for a ride in it?'

'No, thanks. I've got homework to do,' said Tim.

'I'll be seeing you again, Iseult. May I come again tomorrow?' asked Charles as he slid into the driving seat.

'If you wish,' she said noncommittally.

He turned on the ignition, released the brake and the little car shot forward and roared down the driveway.

'What was he doing here?' demanded Tim. He was frowning fiercely.

'Visiting. What do you have for homework?'

'Beastly old spelling,' Tim growled as they moved off. 'I don't like him, even if he is my cousin. And I bet Dad wouldn't like it if he knew Charles had been visiting you and was coming again tomorrow.'

'Don't be silly,' Iseult rebuked him laughingly. 'I'm sure your father won't mind when I tell him his cousin has been visiting us while he's been away.'

'How long before he comes home, Isa?'

'Another week and he'll be here.'

'Great! Then he'll be able to come to the school sports day and see me run.' Tim's frown had gone and he skipped into the house, his jealousy of Charles forgotten.

CHAPTER SIX

'I HEAR you've been having a daily visitor, male variety.' Win's voice was lightly mocking and Iseult gave her a wary glance. They were both in the gallery on the High Street in Polruth and Iseult was printing a card with the name and price of a watercolour which she had just brought in to hang.

'You mean Charles Marriott?' she said. 'Yes, he's called several times. Who told you?'

'Tim, of course, and also Mark, who'd noticed the sports car going up and down the drive most afternoons recently. How long has Charles been at the Cove?'

'About two weeks. Tim and I met him when we sailed over to Potter's Pyll. He's in hiding, he says, to write a play about this district.'

'So he was telling Mark. He called in at the gatehouse one day to ask Mark if he had any books on the history of the china clay industry. He wanted information about the families which were engaged in exporting the clay from Polruth.' Win glanced at Iseult mockingly. 'I wonder if his visits to you come under the heading of research too?'

'I don't think so. He's just being friendly,' replied Iseult coolly. 'And I can hardly turn him away from the door of Linyan, can I? He's related to Nicholas.'

'But not closely related. And there's never been much love lost between the Veryans and the Marriotts. They were always rivals in the smuggling trade, trying to go one better than the other.'

'If they were rivals how did the families come to be related?' asked Iseult.

'The story goes that a Marriott kidnapped a Veryan woman, the daughter of Ralph Veryan, I believe, who built Linyan House. He was trying to get his own back on Veryan for some reason. But his revenge boomeranged on him when he fell in love with her and she shamed him into marrying her when she conceived his child. Her father was furious, apparently, and wouldn't speak to her again.'

'How silly,' remarked Iseult. 'And uncivilised.'

'I agree,' said her mother. 'But the feud continued, and even in Matthew's time the Marriotts were never welcome at Linyan House—and I know, because Mrs Tremayne, Captain Matthew's housekeeper told me, that the old man didn't like his daughter-in-law being friendly with Charles.'

'Captain Matthew didn't like Rosita. He didn't think she was good enough for Nicholas and he made her stay at Linyan very uncomfortable, Charles told me.'

'Mmm. You want to take anything *he* says with a pinch of salt,' said Win dryly. 'He isn't a writer for nothing. He has a great imagination and tends to over-dramatise everything. When do you expect Nick?'

'Today, six weeks from the day we were married,' replied Iseult airily. 'And since he once told me he's a stickler for punctuality I expect he'll be here before nightfall.'

'Hasn't he written to you since he went away?' asked her mother.

'No.'

'Nor phoned you?' Win's fine eyebrow's were raised in surprise.

'No. How could he phone me from a ship?'

'Oh, come on, Isa,' said Win critically. 'This is the second half of the twentieth century and tele-communications are in. He could phone you any time he wants from the ship.'

'Oh. I didn't know.' Iseult felt foolish and ignorant. 'Well, presumably he didn't want to phone me, had nothing to say to me. He doesn't have to keep in touch all the time, you know. I'm not expecting him to.' Her lips curved into a mocking smile. 'This is the second half of the twentieth century, Mum, as you've just pointed out, and the liberated marriage is in. Nicholas and I don't intend to live in one another's pockets all the time, nor expect too much of each other. From all accounts that's what went wrong with his first marriage. Rosita expected too much of him. Where do you want this picture hung?'

The question diverted Win from the subject of Nicholas as Iseult hoped it would and nothing more was said about him for the rest of the afternoon. When Iseult had finished helping her mother she drove up to the school to collect Tim and some of his friends who lived in the direction of Linyan, and drove them home. Nicholas wasn't in the house and by dusk he hadn't arrived, nor had he phoned to say he was on his way or to ask her to pick him up somewhere.

'You said he'd be back today,' Tim was noisy in his disappointment when she sent him to bed. 'You said he'd be back in time for sports day, and that's Thursday.'

'I know I did,' said Iseult with a sigh. Another lesson learned, she thought ruefully. She should not have been so specific about the date of Nicholas's return. 'Perhaps he'll come tomorrow.'

But he didn't come. All day she stayed in the house expecting the phone to ring, but it didn't, and she found herself walking from room to room anxiously peering from windows, hoping to see a taxi come up the drive with Nicholas in it, wondering how she was going to explain to Tim his father's non-arrival, but the only car that came was Charles's. And he didn't seem to be at all surprised when she told him Nicholas hadn't arrived home yet.

'The usual Veryan unpredictability,' he remarked.

'But he's ... he's ... usually such a stickler for punctuality,' she protested.

'Is he?' he drawled. 'First I've heard of it. This

is the sort of thing Rosita had to put up with. Not knowing where the loved one is when he should be with you can be very wearing, you know. She never knew when he was coming or going. But then I don't suppose that sort of thing will bother you. You didn't marry him for love, did you?'

She returned his mocking glance with one of exasperation.

'No, I didn't, and it doesn't bother me that he hasn't come when he said he would on my own account, but it does on Tim's. Charles, would you mind leaving now. I'd like to go and meet Tim from school. I promised I'd drive him and a friend out to the beach at Trenlivet Bay to swim if the weather was right.'

'I'll come with you,' he offered. 'It's a long time since I went swimming at Trenlivet Sands.'

'No, I think it would be best if you don't come,' Iseult said firmly, looking at him steadily.

His eyes narrowed slightly and his smile was rather wry.

'Oh. People talking about us already?' he said dryly.

'Not as far as I know, but I would prefer it if they didn't,' she retorted.

Going to the beach and having a picnic tea there was just what was required to distract Tim from the fact that Nicholas had not returned home. Since temperatures were up and for once there wasn't a cloud in the sky the yellow sands were crowded with families taking advantage of the warmth to swim or to sunbathe. Iseult stayed there

as long as she could and on her way back to
Linyan called in at the gatehouse.

'Nicholas phoned, soon after six,' Win told her.
'He'd tried the house and couldn't get any answer.
He said to tell you he'd be home in the morning.'

'What time?'

'He didn't say.'

'As long as he's here in time for the school
sports, they start at ten o'clock.'

'I think it will be earlier than that,' said Win.
'He's coming on the overnight train from London.
He says not to bother about meeting the train.
He'll get some sort of a lift from the station.
There's always someone from Polruth meeting the
train who'll give him a ride.'

Glad for Tim's sake that she knew for certain
when Nicholas would be arriving, Iseult slept well
that night, awakening only when she heard doors
being opened and closed on the landing. Suddenly
the door of the room where she was sleeping and
had slept ever since she had moved into Linyan
was opened, and in the greyish gloom of the early
morning light she saw Nicholas look round the
edge of the door. He saw her, stepped into the
room and closing the door leaned against it to
stare at her from under frowning eyebrows.

'What the hell are you doing, sleeping in here?'
His voice was pitched low, so that he wouldn't be
heard by the nearby Tim, she guessed, but there
was an unpleasant rasp to it, and as always when
he showed arrogance she felt resentment rising
within her. She sat up in bed, her movements

sharp, and tossed her sleep-tangled hair back from her face.

'Why shouldn't I sleep in here?' she retorted. 'I like this room, and it's near to Tim's.'

'So is my room,' he replied smoothly. 'In fact, it's right across from his.'

'Oh, I see,' she said coolly. 'You assumed I'd move into the master's bedroom. Well, you assumed wrongly. I like to have my own bedroom. Anyway, that room is awfully gloomy. I hate that antiquated flock wallpaper.' She looked round the small room with pleasure. Its walls were covered with a paper patterned with delicately coloured and drawn wild flowers, its furniture was simple and made from golden pinewood, and its draperies were pale green. 'This suits me much better.'

'It used to be my sister's,' he said. He pushed away from the door and walked towards the bed. His hair was shaggy and needed trimming after the weeks at sea. Dressed in a thick high-necked sweater and dark grey trousers, he seemed very big and tough-looking, and Iseult wasn't sure she liked the way he was looking at her. There was menace in the opaque darkness of his eyes and when he sat down abruptly on the bed, close to her, her nerves quivered uncontrollably and she shifted away from him. Nicholas noticed and his mouth took on an unpleasant curve.

'It's all right, I'm not going to touch you,' he said coldly. 'Did you get my message to say I'd be here this morning?'

'Yes. Yes, thank you. I'm glad you phoned.

Tim has been very anxious. We ... I mean, I thought you would be here on Tuesday?'

'Why?' he looked puzzled.

'Well, you did say you'd be back in six weeks' time and since you once told me you're a stickler for punctuality I thought that meant exactly six weeks, to the day.'

'So you made a wrong assumption too,' he mocked. 'I said in *about* six weeks. Actually we did dock on Tuesday and I left the ship then, but I decided to go up to London to see a friend before coming down here.'

'You could have let us know on Tuesday,' she rebuked him. 'Then Tim wouldn't have been so disappointed when you didn't arrive.'

'Tim was disappointed because you made the mistake of telling him when I was due to be home,' he retorted. 'Anyway, he'll soon get over his disappointment when he sees what I've brought home for him; when he knows why I was delayed. It's downstairs in a basket.'

'A puppy?' she guessed.

'That's right. A Labrador. My friend near London breeds them. I phoned him from the ship when we docked and he said he had one that seemed to be the right age and sex for Tim, so I went straight away to see it.'

'Oh, let's go and wake Tim,' Iseult said eagerly, pushing back the bedclothes and slipping out the other side of the single bed. She picked up her dressing gown from the chair where she had left it and pulled it on and zipped it up. 'It's time he was getting up for school anyway.'

On her way to the bedroom door she found
Nicholas in her way. Plunging her hands into the
slit pockets of her robe, she squared up to him,
head back, chin tilted, her glance cool and steady.

'It's good to see you, Iseult,' he drawled, his
glance directed to her mouth. 'Aren't you glad
I've come home?'

'Yes, of course I am.'

'You might show that you are.' He raised his
eyes to hers and she felt a shock go through her
when she saw they were glittering with anger.

'Oh, very well,' she sighed, and tilted one cheek
towards him. Nothing happened, but she heard
his breath come out in a savage hiss.

'Is that the best you have to offer?' His voice
rasped her nerves like a steel file.

'Yes, it is,' she retorted. 'At this time of day when
I have other more important matters on my mind.'

'Then you can keep it!' he snarled. He swung
round, flung open the door, strode out and along
the landing to Tim's room, leaving her feeling as
if he had just struck the cheek she had offered
him even though he hadn't touched her.

Tim was ecstatic about the puppy and immediately named it Goldie because of the colour
of its hair. The boy's excitement and his subsequ-
ent chatter lasted all through breakfast and he
didn't seem to notice that Nicholas and Iseult
were more than usually silent, ignoring each other
deliberately.

'Will you bring him with you when you come

to watch the sports?' Tim asked Nicholas pleadingly as he prepared to go to school.

'I suppose I'll have to,' shrugged Nicholas.

'I want to show him to my friends,' said Tim.
'You're coming to watch me run too, aren't you,
Isa?'

I. . . .' she began, having decided that she would
find some reason for not going because she didn't
want to be with Nicholas.

'Of course she is,' said Nicholas curtly, rising
to his feet. 'Goldie and I will walk down the drive
to see you on to the bus,' he added, going over to
the puppy and slipping a leash on to its collar. 'I
expect it's time he went for a walk.'

The school sports were held in a field behind
the school building and were watched mostly by
mothers of the children participating, although
there were a few fathers in attendance like
Nicholas. Tim didn't win either of his races. He
didn't even get a place, and in the last one he fell
over, grazing his knee, so that he had to be taken
into the school to have it cleaned and bandaged.

When the sports were over at twelve-thirty
Nicholas took them for lunch at a fish restaurant
near the wharf. When she had finished eating
Iseult rose to her feet determinedly.

'You can take Tim back to school,' she said
coolly. 'I'm going to help Mother at the gallery.
I've been doing that every afternoon lately. It
gives her a break.'

'What time will you be back at Linyan?' said
Nicholas.

'Oh, about five or five-thirtyish. There isn't any real rush for me to get back now that you're home and can look after Tim, is there?' She smiled with false sweetness at him. 'Don't bother to come and pick me up. Mother will drive me back to Linyan.'

'All right.' He shrugged indifferently, not looking at her. 'We'll see you later.'

His casual attitude irritated her as much as it had done before they had been married. But then did she prefer it when he behaved arrogantly, imposing his will on her? Iseult wondered as she stalked out of the restaurant and made her way to the steep, narrow stair-stepped main street. Sunlight glittered on the whitewashed walls of the old slate-roofed buildings. Latticed windows were open wide to welcome the warm air. Bright fuchsias and geraniums blazed in hanging baskets. Usually quiet at this time of day because the small shops closed for an hour or so at midday, the street was thronged with people and every shop was open. The tourist season was in full swing.

Passing behind a porter from the Polruth Inn who was driving a small brown donkey laden with suitcases up the hill, Iseult entered the small gallery where Win was busy wrapping one of her pottery bowls in tissue paper and talking to the customer who had bought it.

The afternoon was the busiest they had ever known in the gallery and Win, delighted by the custom, decided to stay open until six o'clock.

'I'm glad you were free to help me this afternoon,' she said as she and Iseult drove along the winding road which led to Linyan. 'It was good of Nick to let you come.'

'Let me?' exclaimed Iseult, laughing a little. 'He didn't let me come. I just told him I was coming to help you and came. Would you like me to come tomorrow?'

'No. Thanks for the offer, though. You'll want to be with him while he's home on leave. How long a holiday is he taking?'

'I don't know. I haven't asked him yet,' said Iseult stiffly. 'Don't bother to drive me up to the house,' she added as they approached the gatehouse. 'I'll walk from here.'

Behind Linyan's chimneys the western sky was sun-flushed to a pale peach colour and the front of the house lay in purple shadow. There was no car parked in the driveway and when Iseult entered the house no boy with shining black curls and an impish grin rushed to meet her. No man with shaggy grey-fair hair, ironic dark eyes and enigmatic mouth came from the study to greet her either, and she felt disappointment chill her. There was no one at home.

In the kitchen, on the table, there was a piece of notepaper with writing on it.

'We've taken Goldie to see Bill Hallam, the vet. We'll be back at dusk. We've had our tea.'

The brief unsigned note set her at a distance in the same way as Nicholas's curt way of speaking often did. Crumpling it up in her hand, she looked round the kitchen. It was clean and tidy, no evidence of meal having been made or eaten left lying about. But then Nicholas had been a seaman since he left school and, living in cramped quarters, had become accustomed to cleaning up and putting away after himself. He hadn't left anything ready for her to eat. But then why should she expect him to?

The silence and emptiness of the old house seemed to crowd in on her in a way that had not happened before when she had had Tim for company and she knew suddenly she couldn't stay there by herself, waiting for father and son to return. She walked out of the kitchen through the hall and out of the house into the sunlit evening. Down the drive to the gatehouse she went and into the homely, untidy kitchen where her mother was preparing a meal.

'Nicholas and Tim have gone over to the vet's with Tim's new puppy and won't be back until it goes dark. Would you mind if I had supper with you?'

'I suppose not,' said Win with a sigh. 'Set the table.'

After eating Iseult cleared the table and washed up the dishes for her mother, then went to watch her father working on an etching in the studio.

'Win says she sold another of your watercolours this afternoon,' he told her. 'You seem to have the knack of pleasing the public.'

'Well, we can't all paint fantastic abstracts like you can,' she replied teasingly, wondering uneasily if he was jealous of her small success. Although he was now recognised as one of the leading abstract painters in the country, that recognition had been slow to come and even now came only from art critics and not from the general public, which on the whole did not understand his paintings and did not appreciate the powerful control he exercised over the various techniques he used. He was a great artist in the truest sense of the words, but he would never be a popular one, and if it hadn't been for her mother's ability to please the public with her pottery, he would have starved over the past ten years since he had given up his position as a teacher of art in a polytechnic college to devote all his time to painting, printing and exhibiting. Her mother had been the supporter, the breadwinner.

The sun set and darkness spread slowly across the sky, and as if in response to a signal Nicholas's car turned into the driveway and surged past the gatehouse towards Linyan. But although she heard it Iseult didn't jump to her feet immediately and follow it. She stayed in the living room at the gatehouse, lounging on the settee watching the weekly episode of a T.V. series until her mother came in and switched the set off.

'Time you went home,' she said. 'To your husband,' she added pointedly.

A half-moon silvered the slated roof of Linyan House, but no light shone out from the windows. Inside everything was quiet, yet Iseult knew Nicholas and Tim had come home because the car was outside. Going quickly up the stairs, she pushed open the door of Tim's room. He was fast asleep in bed and in its basket on the floor beside the bed the golden puppy was also fast asleep.

Where then was Nicholas? In bed too? Outside the doorway of the big bedroom which was slightly open she hesitated for a moment, then pushed the door open further. The hinges creaked slightly and she froze for a moment. When there was no reaction to the noise she stepped into the room. The curtains had not been pulled across the windows and moonlight shone on the glossy surface of the furniture and silvered the white pillows on the bed, revealing clearly the dark shape of a head on one of the pillows. In the silence she could hear the regular breathing of someone who was asleep.

Quietly she withdrew from the room and went to her own, closing the door after her. For a while she leaned against the door struggling with confusing emotions; disappointment because Nicholas had not stayed up waiting for her to return home conflicting with relief because he hadn't been waiting for her; and most disconcerting of all, an overwhelming urge to go back to his room, to throw off all her clothing and to slide into bed beside him, press her cool body against his warmth and tempt him to make love to her. Like a real wife would.

This strong physical desire was something she had never experienced before, not even with Pierre, and she couldn't understand why she was feeling it now for a man she didn't love. For most of the night she tossed and turned sleeplessly writhing in torment, not knowing how to deal with new aggravating sensations which were causing her to tingle all over, wishing the door would open and Nicholas would come in as he had the night they had spent in the Hampshire Inn to kiss her and caress her, she didn't care how violently, as long as he came and showed he wanted her. It was his indifference that was so galling.

She fell asleep suddenly, only to be awakened— it seemed like only a few minutes later—by a thudding noise, as if someone had dropped something heavy. Daylight was trickling through the curtains and the clock on the bedside table said it was seven-thirty. Time Tim was up and getting ready for school. It wasn't until she was out of bed and pulling on her robe that she remembered school had finished yesterday with the sports. Tim was on holiday.

Thump! What on earth was happening? She went over to the door, pulled it open and stepped on to the landing. A crashing sound came from the big bedroom followed by a crisp swear-word from Nicholas. She went to the door of the big bedroom and looked in ... on chaos. The big bed had been stripped of its covers and Nicholas, wearing only a pair of faded jeans, was taking the bed apart.

'What are you doing?' Iseult exclaimed, and in the process of trying to heave the heavy top mattress on to his back he dropped it on to the spring mattress and sat on it, raising a bare arm to wipe sweat from his forehead.

'Oh, so you did come back last night,' he remarked nastily. 'I was beginning to wonder if you'd decided to go back to live with Mummy and Daddy now that I'm home on leave.'

'Why would I do that?' she countered rather weakly, remembering how hard she had tried to stay at the gatehouse and how firmly Win had turned her out last night, ordering her to go home to her husband.

'It's something young wives who are new to the rules of marriage have a tendency to do when they find that the man they've married doesn't live up to their expectations.' he said, his mouth curling cynically.

'But it could hardly apply to me, could it?' she retorted, tossing her head back so that her hair no longer fell into her eyes. 'I'm not expecting anything from you. Why have you taken the bed apart?' she added.

'Because I want to move it out of here,' he growled, giving her a glittering, hostile glare.

'Move it where?' she asked. Surely he wasn't thinking of moving it into the room where she was sleeping?

'Don't panic,' he said jeeringly, sliding off the mattress and getting to his feet. 'I'm not going to disturb the room you like so much. I just want it out of here so I can decorate this room. You're quite right, the red flock paper is antiquated and damned depressing. I couldn't sleep last night for thinking about how dismal the room is with this heavy old furniture.'

'You were asleep when I came in,' Iseult said unthinkingly.

'Was I?' He slanted her a sardonic glance. 'How do you know?'

'I ... I ... looked in to see ... to see if you were here,' she replied confusedly, turning towards the door.

'Mmm, I thought I heard the hinges creak,' he drawled. 'Why didn't you stay?'

'I thought you were asleep,' she muttered, and began to go through the door.

'Hey, wait a minute!' he called after her. 'Now that you're up you can help me with this bed. Come on, take hold of the two loops on the side.'

The mattress was very heavy and he took most of the weight forcing her backwards through the door on to the landing, where they were met by Tim and the puppy. For a few moments more chaos reigned as the yapping pup attacked the mattress, biting and worrying at it, until with a forceful oath Nicholas picked the dog up, dropped it into Tim's arms and told him, the dog and Iseult to get lost because none of them were any help whatsoever and he'd be better off trying to move the furniture by himself.

'He's awfully grouchy,' grumbled Tim. 'He was yesterday too, when you didn't come home in time for tea. He said he wasn't going to sit around waiting for you. That's why we went to see the vet. Mr Hallam says Goldie is a prize specimen and when he's fully grown we should make arrangements to show him. He said that Goldie could earn money as a mate for Labrador lady dogs. Can I have the same breakfast as Dad? He likes bacon and sausage and tomatoes and eggs and fried bread.'

Cooking a fried breakfast was not one of Iseult's favourite occupations, since she didn't care for it herself and so had never even learned how to do it, and she had to admit she was rather ashamed of the resultant overcooked rather crisp, burnt-looking effort which she put before Nicholas when he came down at the table, having been summoned by Tim.

'Hardly a work of art,' he remarked dryly. 'Perhaps I'd better cook my own while I'm home.'

'I've never cooked it before,' she retorted. 'You shouldn't expect perfection the first time.'

'Perhaps not,' he conceded, much to her surprise, and she looked up and across at him. But the glimmer of amusement in his eyes as they met hers did nothing to soothe her irritation. If he wasn't ordering her about or criticising her he was laughing at her, treating her as if she were no older than Tim.

'What sort of wallpaper would you like to take the place of the red flock you hate so much?' he asked.

'It doesn't matter to me how you decorate that room,' she replied lightly, collecting up dirty dishes from the table and carrying them over to the sink. 'It's your room, not mine.'

'So can I take it you won't object if I cover the walls with blue cabbage roses?' he said tauntingly, pushing back his chair and getting to his feet. 'Somehow I thought that as an artist you would have some suggestions to make.'

'I've told you, it doesn't matter to me. It isn't my room. I'm quite happy sleeping in the other room,' she replied woodenly. 'Decorate it to suit yourself.'

Nicholas didn't reply, but left the room, and a few moments later Iseult heard the car start up and depart with a snort of exhaust and squeal of tyres on the gravel.

'Dad's gone to Polruth to buy paint and stuff for the bedroom,' said Tim, coming back into the kitchen. 'Will you come with me to the gatehouse to introduce Goldie to Merlin, Isa?'

'Later, when I've made the beds ... and put the washing in the machine,' she replied vaguely.

It was another warm sunny day and she enjoyed the walk down the drive with Tim and the puppy, but they weren't made very welcome at the gatehouse. Win had already gone to the gallery and Merlin and Goldie took an instant dislike to each other, growling and snapping until Mark suddenly asserted himself and ordered Iseult to take Tim, Goldie and herself off.

'I thought they'd like each other,' mumbled Tim as they trudged through the woods with Goldie, who wanted to stop at every tree.

'Dogs very rarely do like each other if they're not of the same breed or if they're of the same sex,' Iseult replied.

'You mean if they're both boys?' asked Tim.

'That's right. What do you want to do now?'

'I don't know. I thought when Dad came home he'd take us out, to the sands to swim. Do you think I could have one of my friends over to play?'

'Which friend?'

'Jem. He lives nearest.'

'How will he get here?'

'I could go and get him, if you'll take Goldie back to the house.'

'All right, but you'll be careful on the road, won't you?' said Iseult.

He set off and she walked back to the house, was almost there when the car overtook her, curving round to stop at the front door. Tim and his friend Jem, small and red-haired, were in the back seat. Nicholas opened the boot, took out several large cans of paint and carried them into the house. When Iseult walked into the hall he was coming down the stairs again.

'I'd like to have lunch as soon as possible so I can get to work stripping the paper off the walls,' he said crisply. 'I don't suppose you'd like to help?'

'No, I wouldn't,' she retorted tartly. 'And lunch won't be ready until one.'

Now she knew why so many women rebelled against housekeeping, she thought as she peeled potatoes at the sink. Now she realised how easy life had been for her when Nicholas had been at sea and Tim had been at school all day. At home they both made demands, expected her to do everything. And yet before she had lived with them they had managed to get on very well without her.

The dinner of lamb chops, potatoes and new peas out of the garden, followed by rice pudding, was a slight improvement on the disastrous cooking of the breakfast, although Tim did complain that the rice pudding wasn't as good as the pudding he got at school dinners. Nicholas made no comment, but ate quickly and excused himself to go upstairs to start stripping the wallpaper off his bedroom wall. The pale-faced, bright-haired Jem said nothing too, but wolfed down everything put before him as if he hadn't had anything so good to eat in all his eight or nine years. He even said shyly, 'Thank you, Mrs Veryan. That was good,' and Iseult bestowed one of her warmest smiles on him. It was nice to be appreciated.

The two boys went off to play in the garden and she looked round the littered kitchen. All those dishes to wash, dry and put away; the cooker to wipe down; the pans to scour; and outside the sun was shining, inviting her to go outside and play too. To play at what? Painting pictures? Yes, that was exactly what she was going to do, her own thing, and be damned to the dishes!

She was in the vegetable garden where Joe Penrose, the man whom Nicholas employed to take care of the garden, was weeding between the rows of carrots and parsnips, and she was doing her best to put his likeness on canvas with oils when she heard a car drive up to the house and stop. A car door slammed and a few minutes later the doorbell pealed imperiously. Iseult went on painting.

After the bell had rung three times she realised Nicholas was not going to answer the door, so she put her palette down and wiping her hands on a rag went round the side of the house to the front. A woman with reddish-brown hair smoothly coiled round her head, and who was dressed in an elegant summer suit of cream linen was standing in front of the door tapping one foot impatiently on the step.

'Hello, can I help you?' asked Iseult.

The woman turned. About thirty years of age, she had a perfectly oval face which was delicately and beautifully made up and her heavy-lidded eyes were slate blue. Their glance swept rather contemptuously over Iseult's straight mop-like hair, cotton shirt, paint-sprinkled jeans and open sandals.

'Are you the housekeeper?' she asked, raising her finely plucked eyebrows in faint surprise.

'I suppose I am,' replied Iseult lightly, feeling herself stiffen in reaction to the woman's haughty attitude.

'Then perhaps you can tell me if Mr Veryan is at home. Mr Nicholas Veryan.'

'Yes, he is,' replied Iseult coolly.

'I'd like to see him,' snapped the woman impatiently. 'Would you be good enough to tell him I'm here?'

'I might, if you'll give me your name,' said Iseult, moving towards the door.

'You look familiar,' drawled the woman, and smiled suddenly and attractively, showing two dimples, one in each cheek, and in that moment Iseult recognised her.

'I'm Iseult, Tris Severn's younger sister,' she said. 'And you're Joanna—Joanna Trethowyn.'

'Joanna Carlson now.' The slate blue eyes narrowed and looked Iseult up and down again. 'Are you really the housekeeper here?'

'Yes, I'm really the housekeeper,' replied Iseult mischievously. 'Won't you come in and wait in the study while I find. . . .' she paused, then added wickedly, 'Mr Veryan.'

CHAPTER SEVEN

HAVING shown Joanna into the study and seen her seated, Iseult left the room and went out into the hall towards the stairs. About to go up them she stopped, one hand on the banister. She was tempted to pretend that Nicholas had gone out, to go back into the study and tell Joanna she couldn't find him in the house, so she hesitated with one foot on the bottom stair. From outside came the shouts of the boys and the occasional thump of a foot hitting a ball as they played on the lawn. From upstairs came the sound of music being played on the transistor radio that Nicholas had with him in the bedroom.

But if she told Joanna Nicholas wasn't in the house there was a possibility the woman might wait until he returned. No, it was better to go and tell him and let him handle the situation in his own way.

He was still stripping the thick paper from the walls, working without a shirt on and whistling the song that was being sung on the radio. Iseult went over to the radio and turned it down. He turned and looked at her.

'Come to help?' he asked cheerfully, his mouth curving in a slight smile as if he was glad to see her.

'No. Just to tell you there's someone here who wants to see you. She's in the study.'

The faint smile faded. The welcoming glow died in his eyes, leaving them cool and wary.

'She?' he queried.

'Your friend Joanna Treth ... I mean Carlson,' she said tautly. 'She said you're expecting her.'

Nicholas gave her a frowning stare, muttered an imprecation and tossed down the scraper he had been using. Turning Iseult made for the door, but didn't reach it. Coming after her, he caught hold of her hand and swung her round to face him.

'We'll go down together,' he said. 'Did you tell her about us, that we're married?'

'No. She assumed I'm the housekeeper, so I let her go on assuming,' she replied.

'But she knew who you are?'

'Not at first. I had to tell I'm Tris's sister.' She tried to free her hand of his grip and failed. His fingers tightened round her wrist. She glared up at him. 'Look, she's your friend and I don't want to have anything to do with her,' she hissed at him. 'I don't want to see her or speak to her again, and I don't have to.'

'You will come down to the study with me and be properly introduced to her as my wife,' he rasped, his lips thinning and anger beginning to glitter in his eyes.

'I don't have to go with you. I don't have to do anything you say.' Again she tried to twist free of his grasp. 'Oh, will you stop treating me as if ... as if I'm a child!' she seethed, finding herself suddenly held close to him as he twisted her arm behind her back. The tips of her breasts tingled as they brushed against the hardness of his chest. His face was close to hers, his breath warm against her cheek as he spoke.

'I will when you stop behaving like one,' he retorted. 'I have to remind you that as my wife you'll greet my friends and acquaintances as politely as possible, make them welcome in this house....'

'Friends and acquaintances, yes, but not your mistress!' She hissed the word at him.

'My what?' he exclaimed, his eyebrows slanting upwards in mocking disbelief.

'You heard,' she said through her teeth. 'Oh, let me go!'

'After this.' He was laughing at her again, but his fingers were hard and strong as he took hold of her chin to prevent her from moving her head. 'You have paint on your nose again, darlin',' he murmured tauntingly, and then his lips were against hers, warm and hard, probing intimately the moist sweetness of her mouth which for some reason opened willingly, welcoming his invasion. For a few moments they clung to each other, standing amongst the heaps of damp musty-smelling paper which had been stripped from the walls, and the rest of the world was forgotten until suddenly there was a thud, followed by the tinkling sound of glass breaking.

'Oh, what was that?' exclaimed Iseult, pushing free.

'A window, from the sound of it. The football went through it, I expect,' Nicholas said calmly. 'Let's go and see.'

He took her hand in his again, and this time she didn't pull free but went willingly with him down the stairs in time to see Joanna rush out of the study into the hall.

'My God, I got such a fright!' she exclaimed. 'A ball came right through the window where I was sitting. There's glass all over the seat. There were two boys, but they ran off.'

'I bet they did,' said Nicholas dryly. 'How are

you, Joanna—apart from being shocked by the behaviour of my one and only son?'

'Nick darling, at last! I'm so glad to see you!' Joanna surged across the hallway towards him, her arms outstretched in greeting. Becoming aware that he was holding hands with Iseult, she stopped in her tracks, her eyes widening incredulously.

'I'd like you to meet my wife Iseult, Joanna,' said Nick smoothly.

'Then's it's true?' Joanna's voice was hoarse. 'I'd heard in Polruth this morning that you'd married again, but I didn't believe Charles when he told me.'

'Charles Marriott, you mean?' Nicholas spoke sharply.

'Yes.' Joanna sighed, her large heavy-lidded eyes ogling him as she completely ignored Iseult. 'Oh, Nick, why?' she whispered. 'Why couldn't you have waited?'

'For what?' Nicholas sounded impatient.

'Didn't you get my letter, last month?'

'Yes, I believe I did receive a letter from you.'

'I told you I'd be here in the summer and that I hoped to have something to tell you. Well, I have. Guthrie died in June.'

Iseult felt Nicholas's fingers tighten on hers and she glanced at him. His lean face was set in hard lines and when he spoke his voice was completely without expression.

'I'm sorry,' he said.

'And now I'm free and I thought we could. . . .'

Joanna broke off and glanced at Iseult at last, her full ripe lips curving into the dazzling smile that dimpled her cheeks so attractively. 'Excuse me, Iseult,' she said charmingly. 'Nick and I are very old friends. Would you object if I took up a little of his time? There's so much I have to tell that's of a private nature.'

'Not just now,' Nicholas drawled. 'I'll have to find that rascal of mine and ask him about breaking the window.'

'I'll find Tim,' said Iseult urgently. 'You talk to Joanna.'

Before he could make any objection she slipped her hand from his grasp and hurried down the hallway to the kitchen. As she had suspected, Tim and Jem were there, helping themselves to bread and jam.

'Who's the lady?' Tim asked, licking jam from his lips.

'A friend of your father's,' she said. 'Tim, did you kick the football through the study window?'

His dark eyes slid in Jem's direction and he giggled.

'Tim, did you?'

'Yes. It was an accident, though. I didn't mean to kick so hard and Jem missed it. Does Dad know about it?'

'Of course he does.'

'Is he very angry?'

'I expect he is, but he won't be so angry if you go and tell him you're sorry you kicked so hard. You'd better go and apologise to the lady too. You frightened her.'

'Now?' The round black eyes were hopeful,
Tim was hoping she would delay the apology.

'Now. Both of you,' she added as sternly as she
could.

'Oh, all right.' Tim slid off his chair. 'Come
on, Jem.'

'And come back here when you've done it and
I'll drive Jem home,' Iseult called after them.

Hurriedly she ran water into the sink and
washed the lunch dishes, putting them to drain on
the draining board. Then she went out into the
garden and collected her painting equipment,
bringing it into the kitchen. The weather was
changing outside in typical Cornish fashion. The
south-west wind was blowing clouds in from the
Atlantic and she guessed it would rain before
nightfall.

'Where's Goldie?' she asked Tim when he and
Jem came back into the kitchen, and the boy's
face expressed dismay.

'He was in the garden with us when we were
playing ball,' he said. 'I ... I ... forgot all about
him when the window broke. I'll go and look for
him.'

'We'll see you at the car,' said Iseult.

On her way through the house to the front door
she looked in through the study door. The in-
creasing wind, although not blowing directly on
the broken window, was blowing past it and suck-
ing the curtains outward. Quickly she went across
the hall into the lounge, drawing back quickly

when she saw that Joanna and Nicholas were standing very close together. Joanna's arms were about his neck and his hands were at the woman's waist. They looked as if they were about to kiss.

Oh, no! Hand to her mouth, Iseult turned and fled into the hallway.

'Are you all right, Mrs Veryan? Do you feel sick or somethin'?' Jem asked.

'No. No, I'm all right. Come on, let's go and see if Tim has found the puppy.'

Tim came trudging up the driveway dragging the puppy after him by its lead just as she and Jem left the house.

'It was easy to find him,' said Tim. 'He was crying 'cos his leash had got caught round the lawnmower in the garden shed and he couldn't get free, and Mr Penrose had to shut the door. Can we take him in the car with us?'

'I suppose so,' sighed Iseult.

She felt exactly as she had felt when she had accidentally walked in on Pierre and Marie in April, disgusted and shocked, even though Nicholas and Joanna had certainly not gone as far as the French couple had. But given time they probably would, Iseult thought acidly as she drove down the driveway. She wouldn't feel so badly about it if Nicholas hadn't just kissed herself in the bedroom. And she would feel even better if she hadn't responded to his kiss.

If only she could run away as she had run away from Paris in April! If only she could take off in the car somewhere and hide for a while. But she couldn't go, because she had Tim with her and the puppy. She couldn't go because the car didn't belong to her.

She dropped Jem off at his house and drove on towards Polruth. Might as well give Nicholas and Joanna plenty of time to talk, she thought grimly. *Now I'm free and I thought we could....* What had Joanna been going to say before she had broken off? Had Guthrie been her husband and had she meant now that she was free she and Nicholas could get married? Only Nicholas was already married again. *Oh, Nick, why couldn't you have waited?* Joanna's remark had been plaintive, expressing her disappointment at finding he had married again.

Why hadn't Nicholas waited? Iseult frowned and chewed her lower lip, staring ahead at the grey surface of the road, hardly noticing where she was going. Nicholas had known Joanna would be coming to Polruth this summer. So why hadn't he waited for her to come? Why had he rushed into marriage with herself?

For Tim's sake. For the same reason that she had married him, of course. And she had known that had been his reason for marrying her all along, so why get upset because Joanna had come into the picture? Why recoil from the sight of him about to kiss Joanna in the same way that she had recoiled from the sight of Pierre blatantly making love to Marie? She wasn't in love with Nicholas in the same way she had been in love with Pierre. Or was she?

'Isa, it's raining. You'd better switch on the wipers,' said Tim with annoying male arrogance. 'And Goldie's made a puddle on the floor of the car.'

'Oh, damn!' she snapped, finding the switch for the wipers. 'Why didn't you tell me he wanted to go?'

''Cos I didn't know he wanted to go. He didn't tell me,' retorted Tim. 'Where are we going?'

Taking her foot off the accelerator so that the car slowed down, Iseult looked about her in surprise. She was well past Polruth on the road to St Austell. Rain was slanting across the countryside in a grey veil and the wind was lashing the trees and buffeting the car.

Where was she going? The instinct to run away from something she didn't like had been very strong. It had carried her this far along the road, and if Tim hadn't said anything it would have carried her farther. But she couldn't run away from Nicholas in the same way she had run away from Pierre, not only because she was bound to him by the vows of marriage but also because she had Tim with her and she had promised to take care of him.

'I was thinking of going to Trenlivet beach again, but there isn't any point if it's raining, is there?' she said lightly to Tim as she brought the car to a stop at the side of the road. 'What would you like to do instead?'

'Go home and feed Goldie,' he said. 'I'm hungry too. It's nearly teatime.'

Iseult nodded and turned the car. On the return journey she paid more attention to what she was doing. As they approached the coast again the wind became stronger and the trees in Linyan woods were swaying under the onslaught. Joanna's car had gone from the driveway in front of the house, she noticed as she parked the car, and someone, presumably Nicholas, had boarded up the hole in the study window.

As soon as she and Tim entered the house the boy started up the stairs calling to his father. Iseult went through to the kitchen wondering what on earth she was going to give them for tea. She had just put the kettle on and was opening the larder door when Tim came back into the kitchen with the puppy running after him.

'Dad isn't in,' Tim announced. 'Do you know where he's gone? Did he leave a note?'

'No—at least, there's nothing here. Perhaps in the study,' she suggested, and the boy left the room.

Nicholas had gone with Joanna, Iseult had no doubts about that.

'There's no note in the study either.' Tim was back already. 'Perhaps he went for a walk.'

'In this?' Iseult glanced at the windows down which rain was streaming. 'I don't think so. I expect he went with Mrs Carlson. . . .'

'Who's Mrs Carlson?' Tim's black eyes glowered at her from under frowning eyebrows.

'The lady who was here when you broke the window.'

'Why did Dad go with her?'

'She ... well, I think she wanted his advice about something,' Iseult replied vaguely. 'Tea's ready now, so go and wash your hands.'

She let Tim stay up past his usual bedtime because he said he wanted to be up when his father returned home, but by nine-thirty Nicholas hadn't come back and the boy's eyelids were drooping and his head was nodding as he watched the television, so she sent him to bed. An hour later she was going up the stairs herself when she heard a car stop outside the house. A few seconds later it drove off again, the front door opened and Nicholas stepped into the house. He closed the door and, turning round, saw her pausing half way up the stairs.

'Going to bed so early?' he queried softly, coming to the bottom of the stairs.

'Yes. I'm tired. Goodnight,' she said crisply, and went quickly up the rest of the stairs.

She prepared for bed and was drifting off to sleep when she remembered his bed was in pieces on the landing. Where, then, was he going to sleep tonight? Did he hope to sleep with her? Would he come walking into the room in a few minutes without being invited? Not if she could help it. Sliding out of bed, she tiptoed to the door, closed it quietly and turned the key in the lock.

By next morning the wind had died down and thick fog shrouded the sea and hung ghostlike about the trees. His manner cool and businesslike, Nicholas cooked breakfast for himself and Tim and then went upstairs to finish stripping the paper off the walls of his bedroom. After a while Tim and the puppy followed him, ostensibly to help him. Fifteen minutes later they were downstairs again, chased there by Nicholas and ordered by him not to enter his room again until he had finished decorating it.

'Can I go and fetch Jem again to play?' Tim asked Iseult. 'It's very boring being with grown-ups all the time.'

'As long as you promise not to break any more windows,' Iseult cautioned him.

'I promise,' he said, and went off to get his friend.

He was back again in half an hour with Jem and they settled down in the kitchen to play a guessing game. Having discovered that the larder was almost bare of food, Iseult decided to go into Polruth to shop. She went upstairs to change her clothes and looked in on Nicholas to tell him where she was going. He didn't pause in what he was doing to look round, but merely nodded and said, 'Okay,' casually as if he didn't care where she went or even if she came back.

'Tim is staying here. Jem is over to play with him,' she said. 'I'll be back around one o'clock.'

Again the nod and the casual answer. As usual his indifference annoyed her and she marched out of the room without another word. Yet yesterday he hadn't been like that, she thought as she drove towards Polruth. Yesterday when she had gone to tell him he had a visitor he had kissed her and had caressed her tenderly and lovingly as if ... as if ... well, almost as if he liked having her around.

The change in him was due to Joanna, she was sure. The woman he had known for so long had stepped back into his life and he was wishing that he hadn't married Iseult in such a hurry. Yes, that was why he was different. Now he was wishing she wasn't around and that he hadn't married her. *Marry in haste and repent at leisure.* The old adage sang through her mind bringing her no comfort at all. What a mess if it were true! And how could she get out of it? What could she do to release Nicholas and herself from the knot that tied them to each other and which had been tied such a short time ago?

The fog was beginning to lift when she reached Polruth and yellow sunshine was filtering through to gleam on the slate roofs and granite walls of the old houses. Tourists who had stayed the night in the many small private boarding houses and the two public inns were beginning to move about the narrow streets, stepping carefully on the cobbles which were still slippery from the wet clinging fog. Fortunately the small supermarket was not yet busy and Iseult was able to do her shopping fairly quickly. When she had loaded her car with her packages she walked back down the High Street intending to go into the gallery to see her mother. She was passing The Gables, a tall house on the corner of the High Street and one of the narrow alleyways, when the door of the house opened and Joanna appeared.

'Good morning, Iseult.' Joanna's dazzling smile was very much in evidence. 'You're out and about early this morning. Have you finished shopping?'

'Yes, I have.'

'Then come in and have a cup of coffee. It's just perking.'

'I . . . I really don't think I should,' said Iseult, glancing at her watch. It was quarter past eleven.

'Why not? I want to ask you all about Tris, where he is and what he's doing. He and I were such good friends, and I often think about him. Please come in.'

'I can't stay for long, 'said Iseult, going up the steps. 'I have to get back to Linyan to get lunch.'

'Mmm, quite the busy housekeeper,' remarked Joanna lightly as she closed the door. Her long reddish-brown hair was coiling attractively about her shoulders this morning and she was dressed in a full-skirted, tight-waisted housecoat made from sky-blue quilted material. There was about her a complacent, self-satisfied look as if she had slept well and was pleased with life because it was unfolding the way she wanted it to unfold.

She led Iseult through the narrow hallway into the small sitting room at the back of the house and told her to sit down while she fetched the coffee. Alone for a few minutes, Iseult looked curiously around the room. It was cosily furnished with fairly modern furniture. The walls were painted pale green and pretty frilled net curtains screened the windows.

'I thought you let the house after your grandmother died,' she said to Joanna when the other woman brought the coffee tray in.

'The two upper storeys were always let, even in my grandmother's time,' replied Joanna serenely, putting the tray down on the long coffee table and seating herself on the settee. 'I let this ground floor apartment only when I don't want to use it for myself. The people who have had it for the past five years moved out at the end of April and since I knew I would be here during the summer I didn't let it again. Do you take sugar?'

'No, thanks.'

Iseult took the offered cup of coffee and helped herself to a chocolate wholemeal biscuit. Picking up her own cup of coffee, Joanna leaned back and smiled at her.

'And now tell me all about Tris,' she said. Her voice, soft and interested, had lost its Cornish accent over the years she had spent living in London.

Iseult told her briefly where Tris was and what he was doing, and Joanna gave a little shiver.

'*Brr!* Makes me feel cold just to think about the Arctic,' she remarked. 'Is he married yet?'

'Oh, yes. He married two years ago. Mother and Dad went out to the wedding in Edmonton, Alberta. He and Nancy, his wife, have a baby girl now.'

'I see. And what about yourself? I was really surprised yesterday when I learned you'd married Nick Veryan. What on earth made a nice, fresh young woman like you rush into marriage to a widower with an eight-year-old imp of a son?'

'Tim needs someone to look after him while Nicholas is away at sea. He wasn't very happy at boarding school,' replied Iseult woodenly.

'And that's the only reason you married Nick?'

'Yes. It's a business arrangement with mutual benefits.' Iseult kept her glance down on the coffee in her cup. Joanna set her own cup and saucer down on the table and getting to her feet paced rather restlessly up and down the room.

'I can't understand why Nick acted so quickly. He knew I was coming here this summer. If only he'd waited a few weeks,' she muttered, pausing by the window to look through the net curtains at the slanting roofs and crooked chimneypots which seemed to be falling down the hillside towards the harbour where smooth water shone in the now bright sunlight.

'Waited for what?' asked Iseult.

'For me to come, of course.' Joanna swung round. Her normally smooth and smiling face was taut now. Her mouth was set into a thin red line and her large eyes had lost their subtle 'come-to-bed' expression and were a hard cold blue. 'You must know about Nick and me,' she continued. 'We've been lovers, off and on, for years, meeting whenever we could in spite of the fact that he married that silly little Brazilian woman Rosita.'

'And in spite of the fact that you yourself were married too,' remarked Iseult.

'I married Guthrie Carlson for the same reason you married Nick,' retorted Joanna. 'It was a business arrangement. He needed a wife to be a hostess when he entertained his business associates and to accompany him on his trips abroad, to supervise the running of his house in London as well as his country estate.' Joanna sighed and turned to look out of the window again. 'He became very ill this year. I knew he'd die. And his death, when it came, was a blessed release from pain for him.' She sighed again. 'If Nick had waited until I came to Polruth we could have been married and I could have looked after Tim for him. But he's always been too impatient, and now he's regretting having rushed into marriage with you.' Joanna turned towards Iseult again. 'He told me so last night,' she went on softly. 'His actual words were "I'd give anything to undo what I did in May." Hasn't he said anything to you this morning?'

'No.' Iseult licked dry lips, remembering Nicholas's coolness at the breakfast table. He didn't have to say anything to her. His aloof manner had told her much more than words how he was feeling. She placed her empty cup on the table and stood up.

'I must go,' she muttered.

'But you will do something,' said Joanna urgently, stepping in front of her. 'You'll do something to end your marriage to Nick so he and I can be married ... at last?'

'What can I do?' exclaimed Iseult.

'You can divorce him. Or give him reason to divorce you.'

'But we've only been married six weeks!'

'Then it should be easy enough. No doubt you can claim that the marriage hasn't been consummated,' suggested Joanna, her eyes narrow and watchful.

'Oh, I couldn't. I can't. . . .' cried Iseult, turning and making for the door, hoping Joanna hadn't seen the betraying rush of blood to her cheeks. Down the narrow hallway she went towards the front door. With her hand on the knob ready to turn it she paused and looked back at Joanna, who had followed. 'Thank you for the coffee,' she said dully.

'You're welcome,' replied Joanna smoothly. 'And tell Nick I hope to see him tomorrow as we planned. Goodbye.'

Down the steps into the bustling high street Iseult almost tumbled in her haste to get away from The Gables. Blindly she made her way up the street back to the car-park at the top, not wanting to call in at the gallery while she was in such an upset state. Not wanting to go back to Linyan either. Not yet—not until she had calmed down and was able to face Nicholas coolly and was able to tell him she wanted a divorce because of his adultery with Joanna.

She had just inserted the key in the lock of the car door when she heard someone call to her. Looking round, she saw Charles approaching her, gaudily dressed as usual in a violently patterned shirt and bright red jeans.

'Well met, fair Iseult,' he said gaily as he came

up to her, but his cheerful grin faded quickly and his eyes narrowed as they focussed on her face. 'What's the matter? You look as if someone has just given you a body-blow.'

'Oh, I'm all right,' she said breathlessly. 'I came up the hill too fast, that's all.'

'I was thinking of driving out to Linyan after I'd had some lunch. Is Nick home yet?'

'Yes. He came the day before yesterday. He's busy decorating at the moment.'

'Tim not with you?'

'No. He stayed with Nick.'

'So you could stay and have lunch with me at the inn?' he said. 'I've a lot to tell you about the play. I've almost finished it and I was thinking I'd like to go through it with someone. Would you consider coming back to the Cove with me after lunch to read it?'

'I haven't said I'll have lunch with you yet,' she retorted laughingly. 'Besides I'm supposed to go back and get lunch ready for Tim and Nicholas.'

'They can get it ready for themselves. They have done before this, surely. Look, why don't you give Nick a ring and tell him you'll be back later than you said? I'd really appreciate having your opinion of the play and I haven't any time to lose. I'd like to be able to take it up to London next week to show it to a producer friend of mine.'

Iseult thought quickly and decided.

'I'll go and ring Nicholas,' she said. 'From my

mother's gallery—she has a phone there. And I'll meet you in the lounge at the Anchor, in ten minutes.'

'Good for you!' Charles smiled down at her and taking hold of her arm urged her towards the High Street again. 'You can leave your car here and go in mine to the Cove.'

There were several people in the gallery and Win was giving an impromptu lesson in the history of art to one of them who seemed interested in buying the big abstract by Mark, so Iseult was able to make her phone call without telling her mother whom she was phoning. The phone rang many times before it was answered at Linyan, and then it was Tim's voice which came over the line.

'Tim, this is Iseult.'

'Where are you? When are you coming home?' he demanded. 'I'm getting hungry.'

'I'm in Polruth and I'm not coming home just yet. Please will you give your father a message?'

'I'll go and get him.'

'No, no—wait, Tim. You don't have to get him. Just tell him this. Tell him I've met a friend and I'm staying in town for lunch and I'll be back for teatime. All right?'

'Which friend?' Tim growled jealously.

'Never mind. You give your father the message and I'll see you later.'

'But, Isa, what are we going to have for. . . .'

Iseult put the phone down quickly cutting him off, and giving her mother a wave, left the gallery.

Lunch consisted of delicious crab sandwiches and a half a pint of beer eaten and drunk at the bar in the inn. Half an hour later they were in the sports car turning off the main road to St Austell to drive along the side road which curved around the head of Polruth Harbour in the direction of Potter's Pyll and Marriott's Cove.

The road deteriorated rapidly into an almost impassable track over which the little car bumped and swerved and the track led, between tangled bushes with overgrown branches forming archways over it, straight to a narrow pathway. At the end of the pathway was a house, with a slate roof and granite walls like most other houses in the district except that the walls were greenish with damp, the windows were dark. It was a sad-looking place.

'How can you live here and not do anything about the garden?' Iseult exclaimed, looking at the unkempt grass scattered with the leaves of many autumns. In the borders, overgrown with grass and weeds, a few perennials bloomed in a sickly fashion and here and there a rose blossomed.

'Oh, quite easily,' replied Charles with a laugh. 'It suits me fine as it is while I'm in the throes of creating. When I've finished the play I'll probably have a go at the lawn. I promised father I'd tidy the place up a bit in return for letting me have it for the summer.' He opened the front door and gestured to her to step in. 'You'll find it's much better inside, although not as grand as Linyan, of course. The Marriotts were never as well-to-do as the Veryans were, in the past, possibly because they were not as aggressive nor as devious. They were essentially farmers and only turned to fair trading—that's smuggling to you—towards the end of the eighteenth century when a series of poor summers caused their fortunes as farmers to fail. They found themselves amongst the "have-nots" and were glad enough, like other poor members of society, to participate in any enterprise that might help to fill their pockets as well as their stomachs. Whereas the Veryans, who had always been seafarers, were in the trade from the sixteenth century onwards.'

'You seem to have made quite a study of the subject,' said Iseult as she followed him down a dark panelled passage and into a pleasant parlour, also panelled in dark wood.

'That's because I've been reading it up recently. You see, my play is based on the story of the kidnapping of Martha Veryan by George Marriott and the uniting of the two families by their marriage. It's a story of revenge and counter-revenge set against the background of the effects of the industrial revolution on the region, when fortunes were being made and lost in tin and copper mining.'

Apart from the usual armchairs and settee set in front of the wide granite fireplace where a wood fire smoked in a dog grate the room was furnished with an old-fashioned mahogany sideboard, a glass-fronted cabinet holding treasures of antique glass, china and silver, presumably collected by

the Marriott family over the years, and a big
desk pushed against a wall. On the desk was a
typewriter almost buried under a heap of yellow
copy paper covered with lines of typewritten
words.

'I thought we'd read through the play aloud.
taking alternate parts,' said Charles, searching
through the chaos on the desk and finding, sur-
prisingly, some sheaves of white paper, also
covered with lines of words but which were neatly
clipped together. 'Are you agreeable?' he asked.
'It helps me enormously to hear the words read
aloud. I know then whether I've achieved the
rhythm in the spoken prose that I want. In this
case I'll know whether the play has a distinct late
eighteenth-century flavour and also whether it
had the right amount of suspense.'

They sat side by side on the settee to read. At
first Iseult was a little shy of giving the words she
had to read any dramatic quality, but finding that
Charles entered into the parts which he read
without any inhibition as he became in turn the
romantically-minded artistically-inclined, rather
weak George Marriott, George's drunken father
William Marriott and the sternly remote dis-
ciplinarian Ralph Veryan, the father of Martha,
she relaxed and began to enjoy the parts that she
read. In turn she was the strong-willed, fiery-
tempered Martha Veryan and the local fisherman's daughter Mary Trenwith who had been
desperately in love with George.

To her surprise it took them almost two hours

to read the three-act play, and by the time they had finished the tide had turned and she could see the water swirling up over the rocks on the beach.

'So what do you think of it?' asked Charles, leaning back against the back of the sofa. 'Is there enough suspense? Will it hold the attention of a theatre audience?'

'You've caught the atmosphere of evil very well,' replied Iseult. 'And I can hardly wait to know what's going to happen in the end.'

'Well, I suppose you know that in reality Martha Veryan triumphed and shamed George Marriott into marrying her, then persuaded him to emigrate with her.'

'Where did they go?'

'Only to England,' said Charles with a grin. 'But in those days to leave Cornwall and go to live in another part of Britain was regarded by people born and bred here as emigration to a foreign land. They went to London and through Martha's determination they prospered fairly well. My father is their direct descendant. Old William stayed on here with his younger son Jeremiah who inherited the farm. but Jeremiah's children all died young and when he passed on this property was taken over by the London Marriotts. They kept it as a holiday house, visiting it only in the summer.'

'What happened to Mary Trenwith?'

'I'm not sure. But I thought I would have her die in the play from unrequited love.' Charles broke off, frowning. 'Sounds as if we have a visitor, coming in a four-wheel vehicle,' he remarked, and rose to his feet. Iseult looked at her watch and also stood up.

'I'd better go back to Polruth. It's after four,' she said, following him into the passageway.

'You'll have a cup of tea first, though,' said Charles, just as someone banged the brass knocker on the front door. Charles opened the door. On the step, seeming to tower over Charles, darkly silhouetted against the afternoon sunshine, stood Nicholas.

CHAPTER EIGHT

STILL under the influence of Charles's dark and dramatic play, Iseult half expected Nicholas to behave like Ralph Veryan had behaved when he had come looking for his daughter Martha; to stalk into the house, pushing Charles aside, to snap his riding whip against his boots and to demand in a harsh, arrogant voice for Martha to be returned to him. Instead he stayed where he was on the doorstep, hands pushed casually into his trouser pockets, and spoke coolly.

'Hello, Charles. I thought I'd come and collect Iseult and save you having to drive her back to Polruth.'

'Hi, Nick.' Charles was perhaps a little too hearty in his greeting as he held out his hand. 'Long time no see. Come in. Isa and I were just going to have a cuppa. Will you join us? Or would you care for something stronger? I do have some Scotch.'

'Scotch would be fine,' replied Nicholas easily, and stepped into the house, ducking his head beneath the low lintel of the doorway.

'Then come right through into the parlour,' said Charles. He sounded extremely nervous. 'Isa and I have been reading the play I've written. She's been a great help. Would you like something stronger than tea now, Isa?'

'No, thank you. But don't bother with the tea. I'll have a soft drink if you have any.'

'Lemonade?'

'Yes, yes, please.'

Charles went over to the sideboard, opened one of the cupboards and took out glasses and two bottles, and busied himself pouring the drinks. Nicholas stood on the hearthrug in front of the fireplace. Iseult sat down again on the settee and began to gather together the scattered pages of the play. For some reason she couldn't fathom she was afraid to look at Nicholas.

'How long is it since we met last?' Charles asked. He was still being too hearty, thought Iseult, as she took the glass of lemonade he offered to her and watched him hand a small glass of whisky to Nicholas.

'About four years ago. You were writing

something then,' replied Nicholas. 'I forget what.'

'So do I,' said Charles lightly.

'Rosita was alive then,' said Nicholas quietly, and Iseult looked up at him quickly. He wasn't looking at her but was staring down at the glass of Scotch in his hand, his lean face impassive, revealing nothing of his feelings or thoughts. He looked up sharply, directly at Charles. 'She used to visit you here sometimes, didn't she?'

'Occasionally,' replied Charles, leaning against the desk. 'She used to come when she was fed-up with Uncle Matthew. He gave her a hell of a time, you know, when you weren't there.'

'And she came to see you the day she left Linyan,' said Nicholas, his voice deceptively smooth.

'Did she? Are you sure? Who told you that?' Charles spoke jerkily, tossed off the whisky in his glass and went over to the sideboard to refill it.

'My father. Before she left the house that day she told him she was going to meet you and go away with you,' drawled Nicholas. 'Did you go to meet her in Polruth like you met Iseult today, and drive her out here?'

'No, I didn't,' retorted Charles. 'To tell the truth, I don't know how she got here that day. I assumed she took one of the taxis from Polruth.'

'Then you admit she did come to see you that day?' Nicholas's glance was sharp and stabbing again.

'Yes,' muttered Charles sullenly, and drank

some more whisky.

'You must have been the last person to see her alive,' said Nicholas softly.

'What the hell are you getting at?' blustered Charles, but was interrupted by a knock on the front door. He put his glass down on the desk, muttered, 'Excuse me,' and went out of the room. The pages of the play once more tidily clipped together, Iseult stood up and walked over to the desk to put them down, still not looking at Nicholas, but very much aware that he was watching every move she made. The silence between them was stretching her nerves to twanging point when Joanna seemed to burst into the room.

'You always drive so damned fast, Nick,' Joanna blurted. 'I couldn't keep up with you.' She gave Iseult a sidelong glance. 'Hello, Iseult. I told Nick you'd be here, and I was right.'

'You didn't have to follow me over here,' said Nicholas coldly. 'But now that you're here you can answer a question. Did you drive Rosita over here the day she left Linyan, the day she went missing?'

'Rosita?' Joanna managed a rather mocking laugh. 'Why are we talking about her?'

'Because I want to,' replied Nicholas. 'Did you drive her over here, that day?'

'Charles, how about a nice little drink for me?' said Joanna, turning to Charles 'Scotch with a touch . . . just a touch of ginger ale, please.' She swung back to Nick and walked right up to him. 'Darling, Rosita's dead and buried, so why bother with her now? Knowing the truth about her isn't going to bring her back, you know.'

'Will you please stop dodging the issue, Joanna,' he retorted. 'Did you drive her over here?'

'I brought her over to see Charles many times, didn't I, Charlie?' Joanna looked over at Charles, who was coming towards her with the drink she had asked for. 'She was so in love with you, wasn't she? Absolutely crazy about you.'

'You know damned well she wasn't,' snapped Charles, glaring at her. Joanna smiled at him, took the drink from him and turned back to Nicholas. Going up to him, she raised her free hand to fiddle with the button on his open-necked shirt just where it showed at the V of his thin cashmere sweater.

'I know I shouldn't have encouraged her, darling,' she said in a very low voice, as if she didn't want either Charles or Iseult to hear. 'But I felt sorry for her. She knew about us, you see, and I thought that if she could have a little affair with Charles she'd feel better, be even with you, if you know what I mean. A little affair of her own with another man, like Iseult's been having while you've been away at sea.' Joanna turned her head and gave Iseult a mocking glance.

'And what did Rosita know about us, exactly, Joanna?' asked Nicholas, his voice purring with menace as he took hold of her hand, removed it from his chest and then dropped it as if its feel was distasteful to him.

'Why, she knew how friendly we've always been, darling,' said Joanna, and sipped from her glass.

'Have we?'

'I like to think we have. I mean, before that little samba-dancer trapped you into marrying her. . . .'

'Be careful what you say about Rosita,' Nicholas warned. 'She was my wife and the mother of my son, and I don't like to hear anyone who's dead vilified. Now I'll ask you the question again. What did you tell her exactly about us. Did you tell her you were my mistress?'

'Perhaps I did. I can't remember,' replied Joanna huffily. 'She was very suspicious of you while you were away. She didn't trust you at all.'

'Possibly because you destroyed her trust,' Nicholas accused harshly, his temper bursting through his control suddenly. 'You always were a troublemaker, Joanna.' He turned on Charles. 'Now will you tell me what happened between you and Rosita that day. What did you say to her?'

'Look, Nick, I feel like Joanna. What good can raking over dead ashes do?' evaded Charles weakly.

'I'm not suggesting you're responsible for Rosita's death or anything like that,' said Nicholas, more quietly. 'I'd just like to know what happened to upset her. She must have been upset about something, and I think you know why she was.'

'All right, I'll tell you,' said Charles tautly. 'She believed you'd been unfaithful to her with Joanna.

It wasn't me Rosita was in love with or was crazy about, it was you, and she was very hurt. She said she was going to leave you, give you a chance to divorce her, and asked me to take her away with me to the States. I refused and told her to go back to Linyan and wait for you to come home.' Charles finished his second drink and went to the sideboard again. 'She cried for a while, then she got up and walked out. I never saw her again,' he added in a low voice. 'But I didn't believe she was so desperate she'd walk into the sea.'

'She didn't walk into the sea,' said Nicholas. 'She walked along the beach to the caves. Right to the end one she walked, but she never made it back to the beach. You know how fast the tide moves into those caves. She was caught in the last one which fills practically to its roof. She didn't have a chance.'

They all stared at him in horror-stricken silence. Charles was the first to speak.

'How . . . how do you know?' he croaked.

'I was out there, for the first time in some years, two months ago, and I found her name scratched on the wall,' said Nicholas heavily.

'Oh, my God!' exlaimed Joanna, and sat down suddenly on the settee. Both Charles and Iseult stood as if frozen. Nicholas finished his whisky, placed his empty glass on the mantelpiece and turning, crossed the room to Iseult's side.

'We'll go now,' he said, coolly autocratic, taking her hand in his firm grasp. 'Thanks for the drink and the information, Charles. We'll be seeing you,

I expect'· He looked over at Joanna. 'Goodbye, Joanna,' he added.

'Nick, wait! I can explain everything.' Joanna looked up at him pleadingly.

'You have already,' he replied coolly, and urging Iseult to go before him from the room and the house.

Branches sticking out from the overgrown shrubs and bushes scratched against the side of the car as it surged along the narrow track to the road, and Iseult was forced to hold on to the handle on the inside of the door to prevent herself from being thrown about, in spite of the fact that she was wearing a seat-belt.

'Can't you drive more slowly?' she said at last, glancing at Nicholas. Under the shaggy grey hair his leaned tanned face was set in grim lines and when he glanced sideways at her the hot glare of his dark eyes seemed to sear her.

'No.'

'I realise you have every right to be angry with Charles and Joanna because of what happened to Rosita four years ago, but you don't have take it out on the car or me,' she protested.

'I'm angry with you,' he retorted.

'Oh. Why? What have I done?'

'You had lunch with Charles and came over here with him to read his blasted play instead of returning to Linyan, but you didn't have the guts to tell me what you were going to do or with whom,' he grated. 'I had to learn that from Joanna.'

'I told Tim to tell you,' she argued defiantly. 'Didn't he?'

'You told him you were going to have lunch with a friend, but you didn't specify which friend,' he replied. 'And why didn't you tell me Charles was staying at the Cove and that you'd been seeing him regularly?'

'I didn't think it was part of our arrangement to tell you everything I do while you're away at sea,' she retorted. 'I don't expect you to give me all the details of what you do when you're ashore in some foreign port.' The car's tyres screeched on the surface of the road when he braked at the junction with the road from Polruth to St Austell and she was shaken back and forth. 'Please will you drive more carefully,' she said sharply.

'All right.' His sidelong glance was wicked and the curve of his mouth mocked her as he changed up to second gear from neutral and the car trickled slowly out of the side-road and turned left, towards St Austell. Slowly, very slowly it picked up speed until they were going along at a sedate fifty. 'That better?' Nicholas drawled politely.

'Yes, thank you. But you're going the wrong way.'

'I'm going to Land's End,' he replied smoothly. 'But at this rate we'll be lucky if we get there before midnight.'

'Land's End?' Iseult exclaimed. 'Why do you want to go there?'

'It's the only place I can think of where you and I can be alone, right at the end of Cornwall and of England. Ever been there before?'

'No.' She glanced at him uneasily. Had he gone mad? 'But what about Tim?'

'I left him with your mother at the gallery and told her to keep him with her until we got back. She agreed to do that when I told her I was coming over to the Cove to get you and that you and I would like to have a few days alone together.'

'Would we?' she asked dryly. 'I can't remember you asking me if I'd like to have a few days alone with you.'

'I didn't,' he retorted. 'I'm taking you away with me whether you like it or not.'

'Why?'

'To teach you a lesson. To make sure you won't forget in future whose wife you are so that you won't get any ideas again of having what Joanna called "a little affair with another man" so as to get even with me.'

'But surely you didn't believe her, when she suggested Charles and I were having an affair?'

'It wasn't and isn't hard to believe,' he said bitterly. 'You didn't welcome me home with open arms exactly, when I arrived on Wednesday morning. And what's a man supposed to think when his bride of six weeks has a separate bedroom and locks her door against him?'

'You ... you came last night ... to ... to my bedroom?' she stammered, glancing at him nervously.

'I came last night,' he repeated. 'And was

tempted to break into your room, and if the door hadn't been made at a time when things were made to last I might have done so.' He sent her another sidelong glance. 'Why be surprised because I believed what Joanna told me that afternoon, that you and Charles had been very, very friendly while I'd been away? You had no hesitation in believing she's my mistress,' he accused jeeringly.

'Well, she was your mistress once and for all I know she still is. You had no hesitation in going off with her yesterday and staying out half the night with her. Besides, I saw you kissing her in the sitting room before I went out yesterday,' she retorted huffily. 'Explain that away, if you can.'

'What you saw was Joanna making up to me, as she always has done to any man who's taken her fancy, as you saw her doing this afternoon. She's always done it. It's second nature to her, and if you'd waited a little longer yesterday you'd have seen me push her away.'

'A likely story!' Iseult jeered, but her voice shook in spite of herself. Nicholas glanced at her, swore softly and slowing the car down guided it off the road and down a tree-lined lane leading to a farm.

'We'd better get this straight once and for all,' he grated, turning off the engine. He swung round to her, his face taut and his eyes a dark burning blue. 'Are you going to listen?'

'I suppose so.' Lifting her chin, she stared away

down the lane and heard him swear again.

'Do you know what I'd like to do, right now?' he muttered in a low threatening voice. 'I'd like to put you over my knee and spank you for behaving like an awkward, obstreperous child!' He took hold of her shoulders with hard hands and jerked her round to face him. Her heart beating wildly, Iseult tilted her head back and glared up at him defiantly. 'But don't worry, I'm not going to,' he went on softly 'I've never hit a woman yet. There's a better way to deal with you.'

His mouth swooped to hers before she could turn her head. Pressing hard, his lips forced hers apart and the tip of his tongue, warm and sweet, touched hers in a taunting, titillating caress, causing her defiance to melt as if it had been touched by flame, and as one of his marauding hands slid slowly down from her shoulder to cover her breast her arms lifted about his neck, her fingers ruffling the thick light hair at his nape. For a few moments the rest of the world was forgotten again, as they communicated with hands and lips their innermost feelings to each other; feelings compounded of curiosity, physical desire, possessiveness and jealousy, all being fused together slowly but surely into love.

After a while Nicholas lifted his lips from hers. They gazed at each other wonderingly yet still with wariness, both unwilling to express commitment in words.

'Joanna and I had a brief affair ten years ago, and that's all,' he said curtly, shifting away from

her until he was behind the steering wheel again.
He looked down the lane. A farm tractor was
coming along it from the direction of the farm
buildings. 'Since then I've seen her about three
times,' he continued, 'twice in London and once
here when I introduced her to Rosita. It was a
short summer affair, when we were both young
and unmarried, but that plus three meetings since
don't make her my mistress. I don't claim to be a
saint and have never been inclined to celibacy,
but the only mistress I've ever maintained
happened to be my wife ... Rosita.' He half
turned towards her. 'Now I have another wife,
you, and I regard you as my mistress too. But so
far you haven't been worth maintaining,' he added
roughly. 'You've been going about with another
man while I was away and today you rushed off
to have lunch with that same man even though I
was at home.'

'I didn't rush off to have lunch with Charles. I
met him at the car-park.'

'You didn't have to go with him,' he flung at
her jealously.

'Well, you didn't have to go into Polruth with
Joanna yesterday evening,' she retorted.

'I didn't go with Joanna. I walked down to the
gatehouse after she'd left, thinking you might be
there. Then I went into Polruth with Mark to the
Anchor for a pint and a talk with some of the
fishermen,' he replied curtly. 'Why did you go
with Charles?'

'I was upset and I didn't feel like returning to

Linyan just then,' she replied weakly.

'Why don't you admit you never intended to go back while I was there?' he accused.

'Because it wouldn't be the truth,' she whispered. 'I thought of running away like I ran away when I saw Pierre making love to Marie and realised that he didn't love me and had never loved me.' Her voice quivered and she paused to control it. 'But when I was reading the play Charles has written I knew I couldn't run away,' she continued. 'You didn't have to come to the Cove for me. I would have returned. I'd have come back for Tim's sake and because ... because I don't break promises.'

Nicholas gave her a sidelong glance but said nothing, and then, starting the engine, he put the car in reverse and began to back up the lane out of the way of the approaching tractor. The car swerved backwards into the main road, then moved forwards again, still going towards St Austell.

'The meat will go rotten if you persist in going to Land's End,' Iseult said practically. 'I bought a leg of lamb and some steak and since it's been quite a hot day they might have gone off already. It would be more sensible to go back to Linyan.'

'I gave all the groceries and the meat to your mother,' he replied coolly, and drove faster.

'I haven't a change of clothes with me,' she argued.

'I grabbed a few from your room when I packed some for myself,' he said. 'Underwear, a pair of jeans, a shirt and a sweater. Where we're going we won't need to dress up.'

'But we'll never get in anywhere at this time of the year. All accommodation will have been booked for tourists weeks ago.'

'We won't need accommodation. We have a tent in the boot and a couple of sleeping bags. We'll camp at a place I know about, where I spent a night when I was on a camping trip with a friend of mine, several years ago.'

'But I don't like camping. I don't like sleeping on the ground,' she argued.

'You'll like it this time—I'll see to that,' he said softly, and her skin tingled with excitement as if he had reached out and touched her. 'So you can stop thinking up reasons why we shouldn't go,' he added. 'You're going to go where I go, and we're going to start living together the way we should live together whenever I'm not away at sea. I didn't marry you just for Tim's sake. I married you for my own sake as well, because I need a wife, a mistress, a lover to come home to. Do you get the message, darlin'?'

'I think I'm beginning to,' she replied, feeling joy leap up unexpectedly.

She thought up no more reasons why they shouldn't go to Land's End. Once again she had been caught by the strong current of Nicholas's will and she was being swept along towards another meeting with the tempestuous passion which she knew now smouldered beneath the cool indifference he often showed to the world. And she wanted to meet it again, was longing to meet it again, because she wanted to show him the depths of her own passion.

Through St Austell they drove and on to Truro, the ancient cathedral city of the Duchy, where the spires of the Cathedral Church of St Mary glinted in the golden rays of the westering sun. From there to Redruth, Hayle and Penzance, moving along with a perpetual stream of traffic, of tour buses, cars and caravans, all going westward to the end of the land.

They stopped at a restaurant in the Gilbert and Sullivan town which is the end of the line for the Cornish Riviera Express train from London and is graced in places with sub-tropical plants and palm trees. Once raided by Barbary pirates, destroyed in part by Cromwell's troops in the Civil War, sacked and burnt by the Spaniards and more recently bombed by the Germans, it was thronged by summer visitors who had descended on it for fishing, sailing, and swimming.

When they had eaten they left the town to drive westward again towards a sky which blazed crimson, orange and gold.

'If you really wanted us to be alone, you've come to the wrong place,' Iseult remarked dryly. Coaches, cars and caravans spawned by the roadside and the famous headland was black with people watching the fantastic sunset.

'I know a place where our only companions will be seagulls and ravens,' Nicholas replied confidently. 'And the only sound will be the waves falling on the shore.'

They drove away along a secondary road that twisted northwards, parallel to the coast. Everything, sky, sea, rocks and moorland, was bathed suddenly in blood-red light as the sun dipped towards the horizon. 'We're now in the hundred of Penwith,' he told her. 'And one of the renderings of the Cornish word Penwith is "headland of slaughter". In this light it seems to live up to that translation.'

'Do you know why it's called that?' asked Iseult, looking about her curiously. Like many places she had visited in Cornwall the area had a brooding atmosphere, as if strange and primitive deeds had been done there. Slabs of granite, weather-pitted and worn, tilted towards each other, rearing up like monuments against the livid sky.

'High on the moors over there are the burial chambers of the first settlers to come to Cornwall, adventurers who came from the Eastern Mediterranean as long ago as fourteen hundred years before the birth of Christ. They came probably from Crete or Phoenicia and were dark-eyed seamen who braided their hair and wore circlets of gold and blue beads, and were my ancestors,' he replied. 'Whether they died in tribal wars amongst themselves or whether they were killed resisting other invaders from Ireland or France nobody can tell, but there are so many of those strange Middle Eastern burial tombs scattered about this area one can imagine that Penwith was a headland where many were slaughtered.'

Iseult glanced again at the moors which were growing dim and grey as twilight set in and shuddered involuntarily. Nicholas noticed and taking a hand from the steering wheel gathered one of her hands into his warm grasp.

'It's all right, lover mine,' he scoffed softly. 'There are other meanings for the word Penwith, too. It could mean "the last promontory" or "the promontory on the left" and have nothing to do with death.'

'You said they were your ancestors,' she whispered.

'I like to think so,' he replied. 'The Veryan family goes a long way back, possibly to pre-Celtic times.' He laughed with a touch of self-mockery. 'Of course, the hot Eastern blood has become tempered somewhat by being mixed with a cooler Northern variety.'

Light hair, dark eyes; a cool indifferent manner overlaying a passionate turbulence. Iseult glanced sideways at him. In the fading light the greyness of his hair could not be seen, nor could the fairness of his skin. He was a dark profile, with the high sloping forehead, the hooked nose, the curling sensual lips and jutting chin of a person from the Eastern Mediterranean.

Then he let go of her hand to hold the steering wheel firmly as he leaned forward to peer along the beam of a headlight which had picked out a small plain wooden signpost almost hidden by furze bushes and which pointed to a narrow track leading down to the sea, and her fancy was interrupted.

'This is the place,' Nicholas said, and swung the steering wheel.

The car bumped and lumbered down the steep track to a small cove where seagulls waded in silvery pools of water left by the ebbing tide. The swathe of firm grass which grew above the shore was still warm from the heat of the sun. After parking the car Nicholas found a place sheltered by rocks and set up the tent. When that was done they sat on the rocks to watch the stars come out in the darkening sky, twinkling above a narrow band of pale green light which curved over the western horizon, the last of the daylight. Beyond that horizon lay the American continent, thought Iseult, places like Canada, the United States, Mexico and Brazil, from where Rosita had come.

'Was Rosita really a samba dancer?' she asked, turning to Nicholas.

'She could dance the samba, but she didn't dance for her living, as Joanna implied,' he replied curtly. 'Nor did she dance with one of the samba groups which compete in the Rio Mardi-Gras Carnival every year. But I met her on Carnival night. I was watching the parade with some of the crew off the ship on which I was serving as third mate for the first time. One of the seaman I was with, who was a little drunk, took a fancy to Rosita, who was also watching the parade, and began to annoy her with unwelcome attentions. I managed to distract him away from her and escorted her to her home.' He paused, then added in a low voice, 'She was small and lost and quite terrified by the attentions of the seaman. In those days I was very romantic and I fell in love with her on the spot. Next time the ship called in at Rio I asked her to marry me, and she accepted.'

Iseult was silent as she struggled with a sudden upsurge of jealousy of the dead Rosita. She hadn't expected him to say he had been in love with his first wife, she realised with a little shock at her own violent feelings. She hadn't wanted to believe that his first marriage had been a love match any more than his second marriage was.

'The biggest mistake I ever made in my life was to bring her to Cornwall to live,' Nicholas said abruptly, his voice harsh and bitter. 'But I wanted my son to grow up to be a Cornishman. She didn't like the climate and she didn't fit in with the people. She was very unhappy, and when I realised that I decided to come home and take her back to Rio.' His voice shook a little. 'I came too late,' he whispered.

Tears welled in Iseult's eyes. The jealousy was washed away in a flood of sympathy. Turning to him, she put her arms about him in a free generous embrace and placed her cheek against his. His arms when round her immediately.

'Why the tears?' he asked, rubbing his cheek against the wetness of hers.

'It's such a sad story. I wish I'd known her. If I'd been living at the gatehouse when she was at Linyan we might have been friends and then perhaps . . . perhaps . . . she would have felt better about living there.'

'Perhaps,' he murmured, kissing her cheek before pushing her away a little so that he could see her face in what remained of the light. 'In retrospect I can see now that it would have been better if she and I had never married.'

'But then you wouldn't have had Tim,' she argued. 'And if . . . if . . . you didn't have Tim . . .' She broke off.

'Go on . . . if I didn't have Tim?' Nicholas prompted, lifting a hand to stroke the untidy tangle of the fringe of her hair away from her brow.

'You . . . you wouldn't have married me,' she finished in a rushed whisper.

'Nor would you have married me,' he retorted, and laughed. 'Strange, isn't it, to think that if I hadn't brought Rosita here and she hadn't drowned, you and I wouldn't be about the begin the second part of our honeymoon.' His fingers found her chin and lifted it. 'I'm glad you married me, even if it was "for Tim's sake", as you're so fond of telling me. I'm glad too that you're different from Rosita and that I feel differently about you than I felt about her.'

'How do you feel about me?' she challenged, tilting her head back, her eyelids dropping haughtily over her eyes.

'I feel as if I've met my match,' he replied mockingly and evasively, and bent his head to touch her lips with his in a provocative kiss. 'Are you going to sleep with me now, in the tent?' he murmured, his breath warm against her lips.

Even then, on the edge of complete commitment, Iseult hesitated, drawing back from him, her glance going to the narrow track which led up to the road, seeking a way of escape.

'There's no escape from love, my darlin',' Nicholas said, taking her hands in his and pulling her to her feet to stand before him.

'Love?' she queried warily.

'That's what I said.' His mouth quirked mockingly. 'I didn't fall in love with you at first sight, fair Iseult, but somewhere along the line I must have drunk the same magic potion that Tristram in the old legend drank, because I'm beginning to love you, and I'm not going to let you go.' His arms encircled her to hold her tightly. 'You'll not escape from me again, my lover. Will you come, now? To the tent?'

'Yes, I'll come,' she answered dreamily, lifting her arms about his neck, 'because I think I must have drunk the same magic potion and I'm beginning to love you.'

In the darkness of the tent on the softness of the sleeping bags, they discovered each other, gently at first, with tender yet tantalising caresses and softly whispered words, slowly arousing the urgent hungry passion that smouldered deep down in both of them until it flared up, a flame in the darkness, fusing them together, making them one. And everything that had gone before, the hurt and regret, slipped away from their minds into the mists of time and they slept contentedly until dawn.

Mills & Boon
Best Seller Romances

The very best of Mills & Boon Romances
brought back for those of you who missed
them when they were first published.
In December
we bring back the following four
great romantic titles.

LAND OF ENCHANTMENT
by Janet Dailey

Diana was a city girl, a glamorous model; Lije Masters was a tough rancher from New Mexico. But they met, fell in love, and were married – just like that. Would Diana now find herself 'repenting at leisure'?

UNWARY HEART
by Anne Hampson

For her family's sake, Muriel had to find a rich husband – and she fixed on Andrew Burke as the 'lucky man'. But Andrew was one jump ahead of her – or was he?

COME THE VINTAGE
by Anne Mather

Ryan's father had left her a half share of his prosperous vine-growing business, and the other half to a man she had never heard of, a Frenchman named Alain de Beaunes – on condition that they married each other. So, for the sake of the business, they married, neither caring anything for the other. Where did they go from there?

COURT OF THE VEILS
by Violet Winspear

'In many respects the desert is like a woman. Anything might crop up in the desert, as in a relationship with a woman . . . But a man can enjoy the desert without getting involved – emotionally.' Duane Hunter's words made it quite plain to Roslyn that there was no future for her in his life. And yet . . .

If you have difficulty in obtaining any of these books through your local paperback retailer, write to:

Mills & Boon Reader Service
P.O. Box 236, Thornton Road, Croydon, Surrey, CR9 3RU

How to join in a whole new world of romance

It's very easy to subscribe to the Mills & Boon Reader Service. As a regular reader, you can enjoy a whole range of special benefits. Bargain offers. Big cash savings. Your own free Reader Service newsletter, packed with knitting patterns, recipes, competitions, and exclusive book offers.

We send you the very latest titles each month, postage and packing free – no hidden extra charges. There's absolutely no commitment – you receive books for only as long as you want.

We'll send you details. Simply send the coupon – or drop us a line for details about the Mills & Boon Reader Service Subscription Scheme.
Post to: Mills & Boon Reader Service, P.O. Box 236, Thornton Road, Croydon, Surrey CR9 3RU, England.
*Please note: READERS IN SOUTH AFRICA please write to: Mills & Boon Reader Service of Southern Africa, Private Bag X3010, Randburg 2125, S. Africa.

- -

Please send me details of the Mills & Boon Subscription Scheme.
NAME (Mrs/Miss) _____ EP3
ADDRESS _____
_____
COUNTY/COUNTRY _____ POST/ZIP CODE _____
BLOCK LETTERS, PLEASE

Mills & Boon
the rose of romance